HARLEQUIN®
Presents

Welcome to a month of fantastic reading, brought to you by Harlequin Presents! Continuing our magnificent series THE ROYAL HOUSE OF NIROLI is Melanie Milburne with *Surgeon Prince, Ordinary Wife*. With the first heir excluded from the throne of Niroli, missing prince and brilliant surgeon Dr. Alex Hunter is torn between duty and his passion for a woman who can never be his queen…. Don't miss out!

Also for your reading pleasure is the first book of Sandra Marton's new THE BILLIONAIRES' BRIDES trilogy, *The Italian Prince's Pregnant Bride,* where Prince Nicolo Barbieri acquires Aimee Black, who, it seems, is pregnant with Nicolo's baby! Then favorite author Lynne Graham brings you a gorgeous Greek in *The Petrakos Bride,* where Maddie comes face-to-face again with her tycoon idol….

In *His Private Mistress* by Chantelle Shaw, Italian racing driver Rafael is determined to make Eden his mistress once more…while in *One-Night Baby* by Susan Stephens, another Italian knows nothing of the secret Kate is hiding from their one night together. If a sheikh is what gets your heart thumping, Annie West brings you *For the Sheikh's Pleasure,* where Sheikh Arik is determined to get Rosalie to open up to receive the loving that only *he* can give her! In *The Brazilian's Blackmail Bargain* by Abby Green, Caleb makes Maggie an offer she just can't refuse. And finally Lindsay Armstrong's *The Rich Man's Virgin* tells the story of a fiercely independent woman who finds she's pregnant by a powerful millionaire. Look out for more brilliant books next month!

Susan Stephens

ONE-NIGHT BABY

ITALIAN HUSBANDS

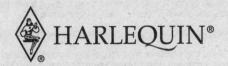 HARLEQUIN®

TORONTO • NEW YORK • LONDON
AMSTERDAM • PARIS • SYDNEY • HAMBURG
STOCKHOLM • ATHENS • TOKYO • MILAN • MADRID
PRAGUE • WARSAW • BUDAPEST • AUCKLAND

ISBN-13: 978-0-373-12655-2
ISBN-10:   0-373-12655-7

ONE-NIGHT BABY

First North American Publication 2007.

www.eHarlequin.com

Printed in U.S.A.

All about the author...
Susan Stephens

SUSAN STEPHENS was a professional singer before meeting her husband on the tiny Mediterranean island of Malta. In true Harlequin Presents style they met on Monday, became engaged on Friday and were married three months later. Almost thirty years and three children later they are still in love. (Susan does not advise her children to return home one day with a similar story, as she may not take the news with the same fortitude as her own mother!)

Susan had written several nonfiction books when fate took a hand. At a charity costume ball there was an after-dinner auction. One of the lots, "Spend a Day with an Author," had been donated by Mills & Boon author Penny Jordan. Susan's husband bought this lot and Penny was to become not just a great friend, but a wonderful mentor who encouraged Susan to write romance.

Susan loves her family, her pets, her friends and her writing. She enjoys entertaining, travel and going to the theater. She reads, cooks and plays the piano to relax, and can occasionally be found throwing herself off mountains on a pair of skis or galloping through the countryside.

Visit Susan's website, www.susanstephens.net. She loves to hear from her readers all around the world!

For dearest Aunty Kat, with my love

CHAPTER ONE

'How soon could I come to Rome?' Kate Mulhoon's fingers turned white as she clutched the telephone receiver. *I'd go anywhere on earth for you, Caddy, but not Rome...*

But even as the words played out in her mind Kate knew she could no more leave her beautiful cousin Cordelia in need of support on a film set in Rome than she could...than she could what? Take the risk that she might come face to face with Santino Rossi again?

An icy blast chose that moment to rattle the office window reminding Kate of another night when she had been working late five years before. But that night seemed like another life, another person living it...

And that person didn't exist any longer, Kate told herself fiercely, fixing her concentration on the computer screen.

'Kate, are you still there?' Caddy said anxiously.

'Just saving my files.'

It was cold in the office—the heating went off at six—and Kate wished she could be bundled up in a woolly jumper rather than her customary office uniform of tailored suit and thin white blouse. She was often accused of dressing older than she should, but Kate had her reasons.

Satisfied her work was safe Kate skipped straight to flight

information. Caddy wasn't just one of her favourite people in the world, she was the film star Cordelia Mulhoon, and as such one of the agency's most important clients. It was Kate's responsibility to look after those clients. She saw all types coming through the revolving doors and Caddy was no self-infatuated wimp. If Caddy called for help, then she needed it.

Without Caddy's mother, Aunt Meredith, to take care of things at home Kate wouldn't have considered leaving the country, but Aunt Meredith was like a rock and wouldn't blink at the sudden disruption to her routine. Even so it wouldn't be easy to leave Kate's litte girl, Francesca, behind. It would have to be a short stay…

Kate brushed a strand of hair from her face as she studied the list of flight departures to Rome. It had been a long day, and a long time since she had last consulted a mirror. Kate wore her dark blonde hair pulled back for the sake of neatness rather than fashion, and the glossy waves fell almost to her waist. She might work in a so-called glamour job, but glamour had passed Kate by. She was a very private person who liked nothing more than going for long walks with Francesca or baking cakes together in Aunt Meredith's cosy farmhouse kitchen. She would plead guilty in a trice to not spending enough time on her looks, and thought her tall, slender figure unremarkable. In fact Kate thought everything about her unremarkable. She was glad of it, because unremarkable was safe…safe from notice, safe from discussion, safe from gossip.

Kate's eyes were her most compelling feature. They were a deceptively soft shade of grey, but it was her gaze that was so expressive, and that had been known to turn steely when there was something or someone to defend.

'I feel bad about this already,' Caddy said anxiously.

'Then don't,' Kate murmured distractedly. She had just identified a suitable flight.

'I wouldn't ask you to come unless I really needed you—'

'You don't have to tell me that,' Kate said gently to reassure her cousin.

Caddy's emotional bank was always threatening to overflow, which was why she was such a remarkable actress. Kate had always been considered the steady cousin, the thoughtful cousin, which had made her break-out behaviour five years ago all the more remarkable. As far as her parents were concerned she had gone from golden girl to outcast in the time it took her to tell them she was pregnant. Only Aunt Meredith had stood firmly in her corner. And now it was Meredith's daughter, Kate's beloved cousin Caddy, who needed Kate's help. There wasn't a chance she would let Caddy down and send someone else in her place, though Pandora's box was a kiddy's lunch-box in comparison to the trouble Kate knew she could start in Rome. Rome was Santino Rossi's home town, and Santino Rossi belonged to that night from the past. By some cruel twist of fate Santino was also the producer of Caddy's latest film.

What were the chances she wouldn't bump into Santino Rossi at the Cinecitta studios where Caddy was filming?

Zero, Kate accepted grimly.

All her instincts might scream caution and urge her to stay at home, but loyalty wouldn't allow her to take the coward's course and so in order to know what to expect when she arrived she delved a little deeper.

'What's happened, Caddy? Can't your manager handle the problem for you?' But even as she asked the question Kate knew it was wrong. What sort of question was that to ask someone she thought of as a sister? Only exceptional circumstances could have prevented Kate from securing the first flight she found. And Santino Rossi *was* exceptional circumstances.

But Caddy was her dearest friend. 'I'm booking the flight now, Caddy—'

There was a gasp of relief from the other end of the line. 'Oh, Kate, I'm so relieved. Marge Wilson has been a useless manager. I wish I'd listened to you in the first place and never hired her. She's drunk all the time, and—'

'We all make mistakes,' Kate cut across Caddy firmly. 'And don't thank me. I know you'd do the same for me.'

While she was speaking Kate's mind was racing. Taking her annual leave from the agency a month early wasn't a problem. She had recently trained up a shadow—a bright girl with all the enthusiasm, thick skin and grit it took to take her place. She just had to keep chanting a silent mantra that Meredith would take care of everything while she was away and that Francesca wouldn't miss her too much. It should only take a few days to straighten things out on the set and find Caddy a new manager… 'Try not to worry, Caddy. I'll be with you in less than a day—'

'I wouldn't ask you to come, but it's a shambles here. And it's not just Marge. Without someone in charge half the crew is high on booze—'

'What about the director?' Kate interrupted.

'He spends most of his time in his trailer with his girlfriend snorting coke,' Caddy explained with disgust. 'Santino's out of town, and we're way behind schedule—'

Santino's out of town? If she had needed a deciding factor that would have been it, Kate realised, feeling instantly relieved. If Santino Rossi was out of town maybe, just maybe, she could get everything back on an even keel and return home before he even knew she had sorted out his studio. 'Okay, that's it,' she said, logging off. 'I'm on my way.'

It didn't take long for doubt to settle over Kate's thoughts. The film industry was only one arm of Santino's massive empire, but it was his most public enterprise. Kate couldn't imagine Santino would be far behind her if he got wind of the fact that things were going wrong on the set of his latest blockbuster. He wasn't the type of man to allow rumours from the frequently scandalous world of film to taint his reputation in the wider business arena. Films might be Santino's passion, but he was known as the Ice Man when it came to cutting deals. He left nothing to chance.

A shudder ran through Kate as she thought about it, and, as if sensing her concern, Caddy started to have doubts too.

'I wish there was some other way, Kate. I wish I didn't have to ask you to do this—'

'Let me see what I can do before you build up your hopes.' Kate was careful to make her voice upbeat and keep Caddy's expectations within reasonable limits. 'With the best will in the world I don't have the authority to start throwing my weight around on someone else's film set.'

Especially when that someone else was Santino Rossi. But Kate kept that thought to herself. This was Caddy's first major role and she deserved her chance. If Kate had anything to do with it Caddy would get that chance. 'Whatever happens, you'll be all right,' she told Caddy firmly. 'I'll make sure of it. And don't worry about Santino where I'm concerned, it's been a long time. Five years,' Kate added needlessly as if either of them could forget.

'If you're sure…'

'I am sure,' Kate said briskly.

'All right. I'll leave a message at the gate. When you arrive just say you're my new manager—'

'Your *new* manager?'

'I sacked Marge before I picked up the phone to you.'

'You did?' A smile of approval touched Kate's lips. It was an unwritten rule that Caddy did any dirty work that had to be done. 'We'll stay in touch. Keep your phone handy and I'll let you know when the plane lands.'

Back at the small company apartment Kate occasionally used when she was working late during the week she stuffed some clothes into an overnight bag. Everything she was taking to Rome was of the rinse-out-and-hang-over-the-bath-to-dry variety, and she didn't plan on staying long. Time was tight if she was going to catch the flight, but that wasn't the only reason her heart was thundering. Thinking about Santino was all it ever took to do that.

It was over five years since Santino and his film crew had breezed into the small English town where Kate had lived with her parents. Five years since the most darkly dangerous-looking men Kate had ever seen had invaded Westbury with a view to using it as a possible location for their next film. All that swarthy Italian testosterone had cut a swathe through the local whey-faced youths. What competition could Wellington boots and anoraks provide to stylish jeans and snug-fitting tops? Shifting eye-lines of uncertain boys to the fierce, full-on stare of a confident Latin male?

It made Kate shiver even now to think about it. It was as if some fabulous circus had breezed into town. It was no wonder the local girls had swooned…no wonder she had thrown caution to the wind and joined them.

Some cruel trick of fate had compounded her foolishness

when the film crew had chosen to stay at Slade Hall, the manor house where Kate had been working part-time as a waitress to fund her studies. She'd had no idea that the tallest and most stunning of all the men was in fact the film producer and Italian industrialist, Santino Rossi. She knew now from the newspapers that Santino liked to remain anonymous whenever possible. That was how he had come to hear her confiding to one of her prettier colleagues at the hall that there was one luscious Italian male for each of the girls—Kate had counted them.

Her own fate had been sealed the moment Santino Rossi had walked up to her and smiled. He had chosen her? It had seemed incredible to her at the time…impossible. And how was she supposed to resist the opportunity of a lifetime? Was virginity so precious you couldn't spend it on a man who looked as though he had been born to please a woman? It had taken Kate about two seconds to decide she didn't want to lose hers to some spotty youth on the back seat of his car. If Santino Rossi was the only highlight in her life and no others came along she would die happy.

But she had been only eighteen, and reckless. She hadn't paused to consider the consequences. She'd been too hungry for adventure.

Kate couldn't even pretend to put a veil of respectability over her actions now. She had been quite shameless. She had watched Santino all night as she'd worked, and when he'd vetoed the bar after dinner in favour of going straight to his room Kate had slipped away and followed him. Snatching up a tray with a jug of coffee and a cup and saucer, she had made that her excuse to knock on his door. Widening her eyes, she had informed him that the manager had sent her up with the coffee Signor Rossi had neglected to order in the restaurant.

Laughing black eyes had suggested Santino knew she was lying, but he had invited her in anyway.

Showing no more subtlety than she had, he'd told her where to put the tray down and then backed her up against the wall. Planting one arm either side of her face, Santino had kissed her in a way she had only seen in films…gently and persuasively to begin with so that her whole body ached for him, and then deepening the kiss until all possibility of stepping back from the brink had been erased from her mind.

The fire that had flared between them that night had been so great that at no time could Santino have guessed she was a virgin. And if it had hurt for a moment when they had come together, it had been worth it for the pleasure that had come afterwards. Pleasure that even now had the power to make her long for his touch…

And it was time that dangerous daydream was over, Kate told herself firmly, locking the catches on her case. Thinking about Santino Rossi's touch was out of bounds if she stood the remotest chance of catching her flight. Taking a last glance around to be sure she hadn't forgotten anything Kate swung her bag onto her shoulder and set off for Rome.

He'd got the word about the trouble from Carlo, the sparks on set. Santino's hard mouth firmed even more as he pictured Carlo, a man in his seventies, making the unpalatable decision to blow the whistle on his colleagues. Things had to be bad for the old man to make the call, which was why he had cancelled all his meetings and was heading out to the film studio now.

He had Carlo to thank for the information that, on top of a negligent director and a leaderless crew, his leading lady's new manager had turned up and thrown her gauntlet into the ring. He didn't need a second warning that everything would descend into chaos if he didn't get back fast.

Santino's mouth set in a grim line as he contemplated what the next few hours held for him. As he never tired of reminding himself, artistic types were unpredictable and difficult. The director he had hired for the film was said to be the best. The best what? Santino wondered now. He would have to fire him as soon as he got to the set. Fortunately he had now been able to hire his original director of choice after the film she had been working on had finished ahead of time. So until she arrived Santino would take charge. Inconvenient but unavoidable.

Receiving the go-ahead from the control tower, Santino nosed his Gulfstream G550 into position on the runway. Opening the throttle on the twin Rolls-Royce BR710 engines, he released the brakes.

Arriving on set, he got the back view first and felt his hackles rise. The intruder was a woman, a very young woman…and dressed as if she were ready to take a pre-school class in her drip-dry blouse and neatly tailored suit. But there was something different about this 'school ma'am'—she had that certain something that made people listen to her. But that didn't stop indignation rising in his craw. Who did she think she was, talking to his people without his direct instruction? There was nothing to recommend her apart from a shimmering fall of honey-coloured hair. In her sensible low-heeled shoes and high street suit, she looked dowdy. She didn't belong on a film set. She didn't belong on *his* film set.

He took some pleasure from the fact that everyone else had noticed his arrival and was standing to attention while she was oblivious to him… She'd get it in a minute.

As it happened it took her less time than that to realise she had lost the attention of her audience. She couldn't have been a day over twenty-five, he realised as she turned around. And then it hit him like a fist in the gut. *He knew her!*

CHAPTER TWO

SANTINO saw the recoil in her eyes as if she had recognised him in the same instant, but she quickly rallied, and held his stare.

It was a wonder he recognised her. She looked quite different now. He wondered what had happened in the five years since their last memorable encounter. He didn't like puzzles. When things appeared different than they should he knew it was a warning.

'This is a closed set. No visitors allowed.' His tone was uncompromising, and he fully expected to rattle her. He expected her to frown, flinch, do something.

'I'm here to protect the interests of my client Cordelia Mulhoon,' she told him coolly.

Clear grey eyes stared back at him without a flicker of fear from a face that was far lovelier than he remembered, a face that made him frown as he processed the visual information. The features were chiselled now, and, however cruelly scraped back, her waist-length hair was still magnificent. Her lips were firm and full, and only her eyes might have been considered too large in the piquant, heart-shaped face, had they not been tinted such a mild grey…

Mild grey? That was a joke! The last time they'd met those mild grey eyes had been flashing fire at him, and those sculpted lips hid pearl-white teeth that could give a man one hell of a nip. Just thinking about it now made him hard. She was a woman he had never expected to see again, a woman he had never forgotten, a woman who by some quirk of fate represented the star of his film, a woman who for some reason had chosen to hide her wild side beneath the deceptively subtle shades of a mouse. Of the flighty fun-lover there was no sign…unless she was playing him like a fish on a rod, of course.

How she was holding it together Kate had no idea. Santino Rossi was Francesca's father, a fact that made her mind reel. The father of her beautiful little girl, and he didn't know it. Only the need to keep her thoughts and feelings hidden gave her the strength to stare him in the eyes. And they were dark, intuitive eyes that could so easily lay bare her soul.

She had never forgotten him. How could she? His face was as familiar to her now as if they had never been apart…the aquiline nose and ebony winged brows, and the thick, coal-black hair he still wore a little too long. The rough shading of stubble on his cheeks only reminded her how good it felt when he raked it against her skin, and his ridiculously sensual mouth brought back memories of pleasure so intense her whole being had started to respond.

It was dangerous to still want him so badly, and there was something in his eyes and in the tug of self-assurance at the corner of his mouth that warned her to be careful. She wasn't the person Santino thought he knew. There was a whole world of difference between Kate Mulhoon today and the girl Santino Rossi had taken to his bed. Somehow she had to make him see that. But it wouldn't be easy when they knew every inch of each other intimately.

'I'm here in response to my client's urgent request.' Kate

held his gaze, determined to keep the conversation confined to business. She wasn't ready to tell him about Francesca, and this was hardly the time. She knew his body, but she didn't know the man. Santino Rossi was still a stranger to her. She didn't know what kind of father he would make for their daughter.

'Very well.' The tension in his shoulders eased fractionally. 'I am also concerned, which is why I'm here.'

He sounded almost reasonable, but would that change when he discovered he had a four-year-old child?

'I suggest we move to somewhere quieter…' He gestured towards a group of chairs the actors used when they weren't needed on the set. 'We'll be out of the way and can have a preliminary chat.'

'Thank you.'

'We will both need to speak to Cordelia in depth,' he said once they were settled, 'and get to the bottom of this problem before we hold a proper meeting.'

A proper meeting? Kate's heart began to thunder. She didn't want time alone with him. She couldn't risk a question and answer session.

It was too late now to wish she had told him the moment she'd realised she was pregnant. Back then she had still been reeling from her parents' rejection, and no sooner had she and Francesca settled in Meredith's farmhouse than a story had broken in the press that had rocked Kate's world. It had stoked the fires of the gossipmongers yet again, making Kate retreat further into herself.

It was said that while Santino Rossi had been in England he had fathered a child. Santino hadn't let it rest there, and had taken the supposed mother of his child to court, exposing her as a fraud. Kate's face had burned with the same humiliation as the woman's family on the day the girl had been discredited, and she had been riveted to the television screen when the shamefaced young woman had been ushered out of court.

Seeing one woman exposed for a gold-digger had made Kate all the more determined to start paying her way the moment Francesca could be left. When Meredith had identified an opportunity with a theatrical agency in London and offered to care for Francesca, Kate had known it was her chance to hold her head up high again and save some money for Francesca's future. She had also known she couldn't risk a long-running court battle with a man like Santino Rossi, and so she had erased him from her life, if not her conscience.

Kate's little girl Francesca was surrounded by the love of her family at Meredith's warm and happy farmhouse where she was untouched by all the ugliness in the world, and she was growing up unspoiled the way Kate wanted her to. As Francesca was just a defenceless child it was up to Kate to make decisions for her, and so now she took the only path she could. She didn't know the man she had slept with. She didn't know what Santino Rossi cared about, or if he cared about anything other than himself. The world of film was a fascinating place, but not all the characters inhabiting that world were entirely stable. Until she knew more about Santino Rossi the man, she would not trust him with the knowledge that they had a child together.

After their brief chat Kate watched Santino on the set. Everyone responded well to him, and had she been meeting him for the first time she might have been impressed. He had reacted as quickly as she had at the first sign of trouble on the lot, dropping everything to come and sort it out. It made her want to trust him, but could she do that after so short an acquaintance? Could she trust her own judgement after what had happened five years ago? She wouldn't risk Francesca's happiness on a whim in the same way she had risked her own.

Kate could feel Santino assessing her in the same way she was weighing him up and felt her face burn when their gazes clashed. How could she ignore the fact that time had only improved upon perfection? Apart from silver wings creeping into his thick dark hair Santino appeared stronger and more virile than ever. He belonged on the big screen, rather than behind it, but she could not allow herself to be swayed by Santino's good looks, or by his blatant sex appeal. She wasn't eighteen now. She was a grown woman with responsibilities. She couldn't allow herself to feel anything for him.

The crew weren't even listening to their conversation, Santino realised, though it should have raised some interest, surely? Whatever she had been saying to them must have worked because everyone was going quietly about their business. Relieved to have the burden of decision-making taken from their shoulders, he guessed. The thought drew his gaze back to her and to her slender shoulders…too slender to bear a burden, their shape was clearly discernible beneath the cheap fabric of her blouse. A quick mental sketch of her naked body lit an old fire that invoked another strong physical reaction, and that in turn warned him to keep his gaze firmly fixed upon her face in future.

He felt like a caged lion. She made him feel like a caged lion. He was used to taking charge; he didn't sit on the sidelines. It seemed incredible to him that a mere scrap of a girl could come in and take over his film set.

A scrap of a girl with big ideas, maybe…

Santino's eyes narrowed as he looked at Kate. He'd had

trust issues since the day his mother had gone shopping and never come back. At six years old that made quite an impression on you. Women were all the same in his experience, which was why he had never married. They all bailed out when they discovered his personal bank was closed to them. But this one was an enigma. She hadn't put all the goods on display with a price tag on her bosom like the rest. Rather the opposite. She had made no effort whatever to remind him of the time they'd spent together five years ago, which, perversely, he found insulting. It challenged something deep inside him that suggested she should make more effort when he was around.

Santino felt a mounting sense of possession as Kate stared back at him. After the night they'd had how long did she think she could hang onto the role of buttoned-up spinster? Her ringless hands hadn't escaped his gaze…

Which was all too much distraction when there was work to be done. Of his director there was no sign, which didn't concern him unduly since that useless piece of excess baggage was about to be fired. But he would handle one problem at a time. His attention switched back to Kate and he couldn't have been more surprised when she seized the initiative.

'I think you'll find everyone is happy with the arrangements I have made,' she told him confidently.

And then she stared at him, waiting for his endorsement of her actions as if she already worked for him, clearly unaware that she was treading on hot cinders around the lip of a volcano.

'It has been agreed that for the next couple of days, or until the new director arrives,' she went on, 'actors will use the time to work on the script while the crew takes this opportunity to hone the technical side of things—'

He was tempted to ask what the hell business it was of hers. 'Really?' There was a heavy edge of sarcasm in his voice, but she either missed it, or chose to ignore it, and she didn't break eye contact with him once. Plus she was speaking to him in the same considered tone she used for everyone else, which grated on him, which made him impatient to exert his authority over her. He only held back because a purposeful air had crept over the set, and right now she had him between a rock and a hard place.

As he stared into those cool grey eyes he guessed she knew where she had him, but that didn't mean he had to make things easy for her. 'Don't you think you should at least introduce yourself, Ms…?' He felt a rush of satisfaction seeing her glance flicker for the first time. The fact that he had affected not to know her, or to remember their night together, had dealt a blow to her pride even she found hard to hide.

'I am Cordelia's cousin, as well as her new manager.' She had recovered and was using a brisk voice. 'Ms Mulhoon appointed me shortly before you arrived—'

She broke off at Cordelia's approach, and as he turned to his leading lady for confirmation he was surprised to see tension colour Cordelia Mulhoon's customarily sunny features.

There was something here he wasn't getting. But he would. And then Cordelia gave a small nod to confirm what their visitor had said was true.

Interestingly, as he dipped his head to acknowledge Cordelia's response he noticed that his leading lady was carefully avoiding his gaze.

CHAPTER THREE

'WELL, Ms Mulhoon's new manager...' Santino switched his attention back to Kate '...we'd better take ourselves somewhere private where we won't be interrupted—'

'We're not disturbing anyone here.' She held her ground and his gaze.

'Don't my cast have plotting and rehearsals scheduled? They should stick to them.' His voice was uncompromising.

'Are you suggesting the actors should work on the set without a director?' she asked him pleasantly, but with an edge of steel. 'Their moves might be changed, and they could become confused. My suggestion is that everyone works on their script quietly for now—'

Somehow he managed to control himself. 'And mine is that they take the afternoon off.' Walking away from her, he said in a louder voice, 'Gather round, everyone. I know you'll all be pleased to hear that I've appointed a new director. Diane Fox will start work tomorrow—' He had to break off as a buzz of anticipation swept the set. There wasn't anyone who hadn't heard of the award-winning director he had brought in to replace the waste of space, no good junkie currently sleeping off his latest hit of the white powder in his trailer. 'Take the rest of the day off and relax while you can. See you on the lot tomorrow at five a.m…'

He glanced at Kate. 'If that's all right with you?'

His gaze might have been ironic, but hers was a little evasive, he thought. And what was with the no-make-up look? Was there some point in scraping back such glorious hair into an unforgiving pony-tail? The last time they'd been together her hair had flowed free and had felt silky beneath his hands…

He wanted her. He felt it like a heat running through him. She had been a revelation the first time around; to see her melt now would be sensational. And a thought was growing in his mind that maybe she could be useful to him…

The film industry didn't respond to the usual rules of logic, which frustrated him. He had been in love with films since he was a boy when they had been the only magic in his life, but it was the finished article that enchanted him. He had no patience for the mechanics of film-making and even less for the people involved in it. This woman had proved she could handle the heat. And she intrigued him. He wanted her close; he wanted to know more about her and what had happened in the five missing years. A business meeting over dinner would give her the chance to answer some of the questions pounding his mind, and would give him the opportunity to propose she come and work for him at his film studios in Rome.

If Santino wanted to give the cast the rest of the day off that was up to him. Kate refused to be fazed by his hard-eyed challenge. As she'd said to Caddy, she didn't have the final word on his set, and for obvious reasons she was keen to get away once Caddy's mind was put at rest.

When Santino had asked for her name she had wondered if he was trying to humiliate her on purpose. But like the worst type of arrogant male Santino gave nothing away. Had he not been a world-class industrialist he would have made an excellent poker player. One thing was sure, the night that had made such a huge impact on her life meant nothing to him.

'You do have a name?' Santino prompted, breaking into Kate's thoughts.

His lips curved in the hint of a smile, but his gaze was hard. Kate felt as if 'humiliation' must be branded on her forehead, hearing him coolly repeat the question a second time. Would he remember her name if she thrust her visitor's badge in his face? *Had she even given him her name five years ago?*

Her face flamed red. There had been no time to exchange names on that occasion; polite introductions had been the last thing on their minds. She had only learned who Santino Rossi was later from the newspaper, by which time he had left England for Rome, having judged Westbury an unsuitable setting for his film.

Kate refocused seeing Caddy hurrying across the set. She had sensed the stand-off and was rushing to her rescue, Kate realised fondly.

'Is it all right if I take Kate away now?' Caddy turned her most beseeching look on Santino.

'Kate,' Santino repeated softly, the corner of his mouth tugging up with faint amusement. 'Would that be wild Kate? Or conformable Kate?'

The Shakespearean reference made Kate's cheeks fire up. So he did remember her. Santino remembered every moment of their night together and now he was taunting her with it. 'Kate Mulhoon,' she said briskly, holding out her hand for a formal handshake.

Santino ignored the gesture and the humour died in his

eyes. 'We'll discuss arrangements for your client over dinner tonight, *Ms* Mulhoon.'

'Dinner?' Kate's breath caught in her throat. A cosy night-time meeting was the last thing she wanted.

'Time is short. You have to eat and so do I. And you'll want to protect your client's interests, I presume? The only available time I have is during dinner. We'll discuss the way forward then.'

There was no way out of it, Kate realised, and as Caddy's representative she couldn't afford to be indecisive. 'I'll need to talk things over with my client first—'

'Eight o'clock sharp. I'll pick you up at your hotel.'

Santino had quickly restored the balance of power, Kate realised, feeling her hackles rising. But it was too late to argue with a man who had already turned on his heel and walked away.

As the two girls linked arms Caddy drew Kate out of earshot of the rest of the cast. 'I wanted to fling my arms around you and cheer the moment you arrived, but I thought I'd better let you establish your authority first. I didn't think you'd want me hanging round your neck. But now you're here—' Caddy gave Kate a hug.

'I don't care what anyone thinks,' Kate said with feeling, unable to stop herself tracking Santino's progress across the lot.

'Then you should,' Caddy argued with concern, 'because there are people in this industry who will stop at nothing to get what they want.'

'Is that what this is about?' Holding Caddy at arm's length, Kate stared into her cousin's face. 'Has someone been unkind to you? It's not Santino, is it, Caddy?'

'No, of course not...' Caddy took a quick glance around

to make sure they weren't being overheard. 'I only hope he knows I'm not involved in the drugs—'

'Drugs?' Kate made an incredulous sound. 'I doubt he's that naïve. You've nothing to worry about, Caddy. If there are drugs on his set Santino will know about them and common sense will tell him you're not involved. What would you have to gain by disrupting filming or risking your reputation? Nothing,' Kate said, answering her own question. 'You're the best person for this role and Santino knows it, or he wouldn't have hired you in the first place.'

'He hired that scumbag director, didn't he?' Caddy threw a hostile glance towards the trailers parked up nearby.

'Everyone in the industry knows he was Santino's second choice. He'd done some good work in the past and Santino wanted the film completed on time—'

'Are you defending Santino?' Caddy tried but failed to hide her smile.

'All I'm saying is that everyone is entitled to one mistake…'

Kate fell silent as her careless words hung between them, and she was glad when Caddy squeezed her arm in a silent show of support. But she had come to Rome to look after Caddy, and it shouldn't be the other way round, Kate reminded herself. 'Diane Fox is said to be the best director in the business,' she said, both to reassure Caddy and steer the conversation onto safer ground. 'You'll be fine once you start working with her—'

'But will you be fine, Kate?' Caddy's voice had turned serious. 'If I'd only known Santino would get here so fast—'

'Of course I will,' Kate said firmly, cutting across Caddy. 'The only reason I'm going to meet Santino tonight is to talk business. I want everyone here to know that you have his full support, and I want you to concentrate on what you do best, Caddy, which is acting. You're going to light up the screen—'

'Do you really think so?'

Caddy was easily distracted and was soon dreamy-eyed.

'I've got no doubt,' Kate said with confidence. 'Holding a meeting over dinner is the most sensible way forward given the time constraints. All I'm going to do is speak to Santino on your behalf, relay any concerns you have to him, and—'

'You make it all sound so easy,' Caddy broke in, 'and it isn't easy, Kate. It never can be where you and Santino are concerned—'

'But this isn't about me and Santino. It's about *you*, Caddy. You seem to have overlooked the fact that the agency I work for takes a huge chunk out of your fee and I'm responsible for you. The buck stops here. It's my job to look after you.'

'But what about you, Kate? Who looks after you? What about your feelings in all this?'

'What feelings? My feelings for Santino, do you mean?' Kate did her best to look incredulous. 'I have no feelings for Santino, and he's made it quite clear he feels the same way about me.'

'Be careful, Kate. You're taking an awful lot for granted.' Caddy's eyes clouded with concern. 'And that's a big mistake where Santino Rossi is concerned…'

His suspicions regarding the morals of the film industry had just received another ringing endorsement. It seemed he couldn't leave the studios for five minutes without some new and potentially damaging scandal occurring. This time drugs and intimidation. Next time…? He couldn't afford a next time. What he needed was a firm hand on the tiller during his absence…a hand not dissimilar to Kate Mulhoon's.

Santino's hard mouth curved in a rare smile as he thought about it. Kate's soft, pale hands had surprised him once before with their strength and ingenuity. If she came to work for him it would be interesting to see how long the new 'ice princess' version of Kate Mulhoon held out.

Meanwhile he had other things on his mind. He had to wait for the police to arrive and take his director into custody. A private interview with Cordelia had revealed that the trouble on the lot went deeper than the drugs his old friend Carlo had told him about, and the humiliation of one of his cast was something he would not tolerate under any circumstances.

As soon as Cordelia had told him what had happened he had called in the police right away. His leading lady had been subjected to a raft of cruel tricks, including silent phone calls, wreaths instead of the flowers she had ordered, manure dumped outside her trailer, and, in one final play of a pervert's repertoire, a particularly sickening brand of sexual humiliation. All of it, he guessed, designed to break Cordelia's spirit in order for the director's heroine-hag girlfriend to take her place. It had been an ordeal for Cordelia to go over it again with him, and it made him sick to think about it now.

An invitation to the director's trailer for a 'coaching session' had led Cordelia to find her 'coach' on the telephone while his girlfriend was busy on her knees beneath the desk… He'd stopped Cordelia there. He hadn't needed to hear more to know she'd been through enough.

Santino's thoughts switched back to Kate. With the arrival of the police imminent and everything back under control he risked her changing her mind about dinner now that Cordelia had been reassured. Kate might even decide to leave Rome before it suited him. Her dedication to her work was his only safeguard. She wouldn't be satisfied he had fired the director for incompetence and drug taking, she would want to know that proper charges were being filed on Cordelia's behalf. He wouldn't be surprised if she insisted on staying on until the new director arrived. But of course, there were no guarantees…

Easing back in his chair, Santino smiled. Yes, there were. Kate wouldn't leave Rome until she was sure Cordelia was happy and working well under the new regime. He hardly knew her, but after seeing Kate Mulhoon at work he could be sure of one thing—she wasn't a quitter.

When the two girls reached the Hotel Russie they went straight up to Caddy's suite, which she had insisted Kate share with her. As they walked in the room Caddy was still imploring Kate to cancel her meeting with Santino.

'I won't do that,' Kate said firmly. 'I won't put you at a disadvantage by allowing Santino to think your advisors are weak.'

'Even at your own expense, Kate?'

'I'll be fine. Listen to me, Caddy.' Taking her cousin by the arms, Kate drew Caddy in front of her. 'This is your big chance and I'll never forgive myself if it doesn't work out for you because of something I've done—'

Caddy shook her head and pulled away. 'Don't do this, Kate. You're pretending everything's all right, but I know you're hurting inside. Look at the tension on your face.' She turned Kate round to face the mirror.

'That's my strategic planning face.' Kate laughed, but her attempt at humour sounded hollow.

'Do you look this strained every time you have a client meeting?' Caddy shrugged her shoulders to show her disbelief. 'You must really inspire confidence.'

This time Kate didn't pretend to smile. 'I'm not strained. I'm just not sure how this meeting with Santino is going to play out yet…'

'You and me both,' Caddy murmured anxiously.

CHAPTER FOUR

HOWEVER many times Kate told herself that it was *only* dinner; *only* a business meeting, she couldn't rid herself of the hummingbird wings in her stomach. There were too many feelings competing for attention inside her: she didn't want to let Caddy down; she didn't want to let the agency down; she didn't want to let herself down, or give anything away. In the end she felt quite sick agonising over the question of whether she could be forceful enough on Caddy's behalf without antagonising Santino, and whether she could get away with sitting an arm's reach away from him across a dinner table without blurting out the fact that they had a daughter together. The end result of all this was that she grew tense and pale and uncommunicative in spite of Caddy's best attempts to draw her out.

'Honestly, Caddy, what I'm wearing is fine,' Kate protested when Caddy held up the latest in a succession of possible outfits for her to wear. Clothes were absolutely the last thing on Kate's mind.

Sharing Caddy's luxurious suite at the Hotel Russie was a mixed blessing, and right now Kate would have preferred to be alone rather than have Caddy see her hand shaking as she tried unsuccessfully to apply some colourless lip salve.

'What about this?' Caddy held out another fabulous designer outfit.

The last thing Kate wanted was for Caddy to think that the meeting with Santino was going to be an ordeal for her and so she pretended to inspect the designer jeans and delicate silk top Caddy was holding out to her. The bright jewel colours were beautiful, but not for her…they would draw attention. 'Perhaps too casual,' Kate suggested gently, feeling bad when she saw Caddy's expression falter. 'I don't know where Santino intends our meeting to take place—'

'It's sure to be somewhere fantastic, and there's a whole wardrobe of clothes here for you to choose from,' Caddy said generously. 'Just take your pick.'

Reaching out, Kate squeezed Caddy's arm. 'You're the best friend anyone could have. And it may surprise you to know that I hadn't even realised we were the same size in clothes.'

Caddy gave a faint smile as she picked up all the outfits Kate had discarded with barely a glance. Nothing about Kate could ever surprise her.

But it was true, Kate reflected. She had never really thought about her figure before. As long as the clothes in her wardrobe fitted she saw no reason to change them, or indeed her casual attitude to what was and what wasn't 'in'. Standing in front of the mirror, she smoothed down the front of her skirt and turned to check the hang of her jacket.

'You can't go out to dinner in the same outfit you wore for travelling,' Caddy pointed out in a last ditch attempt to get Kate to change her mind.

'Why ever not? I had a shower and changed my underwear and blouse.'

'And now it's too late,' Caddy complained, grimacing as the doorbell rang. 'Honestly, Kate, you're impossible.'

Kate's heart thundered so hard she could hardly speak. 'But you love me?' The question made Caddy laugh, but the truth was Kate needed her cousin's reassurance.

'You know I do.' Caddy gave Kate a quick hug and then crossed to the door. Reaching it, she rested her hand on the doorknob as if waiting for Kate's say-so before she let Santino in. 'You can still change your mind, you know…'

'And you know I won't do that. Well? What are you waiting for? Let him in.' Having assumed a bright tone to reassure Caddy, Kate kept the smile fixed to her face—she only hoped she could keep it in place long enough to last the evening.

If there was such a thing as the rhythm of life it picked up pace when Santino entered the room. Kate felt her bright smile falter. It was hard to hold onto her confidence when Santino didn't just walk into a room, he took it over. He drew the eye; how could he not? From her place in the shadows Kate took in the impeccably tailored black trousers and expensive shoes, the chocolate-coloured suede jacket and crisp shirt in bone-coloured cotton. Even in casual clothes Santino conveyed an unmistakable air of authority and she could feel his energy lapping over her. His cologne danced in the air…warm, masculine, spicy.

She watched as Santino Rossi greeted his beautiful star. Santino held Caddy's arms lightly, drawing her just close enough to kiss her continental-style on both cheeks, while keeping a wide separation between their two bodies. He was all male, but he didn't take advantage of the fact. In spite of her reservations about him Kate found that reassuring. Caddy was so lovely that most men were either awestruck, or took the opportunity to slobber over her. Santino did neither. He was confident and restrained, and yet at the same time managed to transmit a warmth Kate could tell put Caddy instantly at ease. That warmth died when he looked Kate's way.

'You know Kate Mulhoon, of course,' Caddy said, trying to defuse the sudden tension. 'Or, my manager, as I should say now.' Caddy started to look uncomfortable. 'For the time being, at least…'

Caddy was floundering, but before Kate could step in to help her Santino made light of the awkward moment.

'Of course,' he confirmed, switching on the charm again, 'Kate and I know each other.'

But he wasn't talking about earlier at the studio, Kate realised, feeling her whole body tremble in response.

'Oh, I'm sorry,' Santino added, appraising Kate from head to toe as Caddy stepped back. 'I must be early. I'll come back when you're ready…'

'I am ready,' Kate told him stiffly.

The look Santino gave her suggested he expected his women to make more effort when he took them out. But she wasn't Santino's woman, she was Caddy's business manager, Kate's steely look assured him.

'We'd better go,' he said, clearly none too pleased. 'Our table's booked. You will excuse us, Cordelia?'

'Of course…' Caddy glanced anxiously at Kate.

Kate gave Caddy a discreet warning glance as she walked past her. She didn't want her cousin leaping to her defence; she wanted to handle this her own way. But Caddy was now gazing at Santino with a dreamy look on her face. Kate had to admit he did look stunning and Caddy had always been a sucker for the prince in a fairy tale. Except this wasn't a fairy tale and there could never be a happy ending where she and Santino were concerned…

It hadn't escaped his notice that she was the same dress size as her cousin Cordelia, and therefore had the whole of his leading lady's extensive wardrobe at her disposal. *Dio,* she could have drawn on the talents of Cordelia's hairdresser and make-up artist had she wanted to. Most women would have seized the opportunity with both hands. Most women would have thrown themselves into this 'business meeting' with relish. But Kate? No.

He took it as an insult. But if that was the way she wanted to play it, so be it.

He seethed all the way to the restaurant, sitting as far away from her as he could. They were being taken in a chauffeur-driven limousine to one of the best restaurants in Rome, and he was escorting a woman who looked as if she had picked out her outfit at the local charity store. It made him doubly determined to crack the façade Kate had adopted since the last time they'd met. The play-acting had gone too far. Who did she think she was kidding?

Luigi greeted them at the door with an obsequious bow, which only added to his ill temper. No matter how many times he told the *maître d'*, 'No ceremony, Luigi, please—' it fell on deaf ears. But this was the best restaurant in Rome, where he kept a business account for occasions such as this, so he just had to grit his teeth and get over it.

Naturally they were shown to the best table in the room. Only Kate's natural dignity made up for her lack of dress sense. The restaurant was packed with every beautiful face in Rome, half of whom he was forced to acknowledge on his way to their table. In a strange sort of way the proud tilt of Kate's head pleased him as she subjected herself to the un-forgiving scrutiny of the glitterati, but that didn't mean he was taken in by her little charade. She could play Miss Butter-wouldn't-melt all she liked; he wasn't buying it.

He settled back as each of them was handed a giant-sized

leather-bound menu. 'Do you have a preference for wine?' he asked her as the sommelier approached. He glanced up when she remained silent and saw her anxious gaze darting about. She looked as if she was ready to bolt. The light thrown down by the chandeliers was cruel and revealed dark shadows beneath her eyes. She seemed strung out as if something big was worrying her. Maybe she would crack a lot sooner than he'd thought.

'A preference?' she said, refocusing on him.

Her eyes were beautiful and he felt a tug somewhere deep inside him when she looked at him that way. Filing it away for future consideration, he concentrated on the wine list. 'Do you prefer red or white wine?'

'Santino…'

'Yes?' He looked up, surprised at the discreet, even confidential tone of her voice. 'What is it?' He leaned across the table anticipating a full meltdown. His eyes filled with lazy certainty as he waited for her reply. He anticipated a suggestion they order room service instead of eating in the restaurant—the same room service he'd given her five years ago. He waved the waiters and the sommelier away.

'I don't like it here,' she told him bluntly.

'That's it?' He sat back frowning.

' I feel uncomfortable. I'd like to go somewhere else.'

He had to admit that where sheer, unadulterated front was concerned Kate took the prize. He had brought her to the best place in Rome, the most glamorous place in Rome. As a rule it was necessary to book six months in advance, and then if Luigi didn't recognise you you were lucky to get a table near the kitchen. What was wrong with her? He was tempted to tell her just how uncomfortable she looked in her ill-fitting suit. 'What do you expect me to do about it?'

'Take me somewhere else.' She held his gaze.

'Like where, for instance?' He gave her one last chance to redeem herself with a little softening of those steel-grey eyes.

'Somewhere traditional and typical of the area…'

Her expression was disappointingly earnest. 'This is typical of the area,' he pointed out in an ironic reminder that she was staying in the best part of Rome.

'You know what I mean,' she insisted stubbornly. 'Somewhere… Oh, I don't know…where *mamma* cooks and *papà* serves—'

'How sweet.' He could barely stop his lip from curling.

'There's no need to be sarcastic.' She gave a nervous laugh to soften the remark. 'I thought this was a business meeting, not a—'

As her mouth clamped shut he raised his eyebrows, daring her to say date, but she fell silent. Looking down, she licked the full swell of her bottom lip. He wondered if she knew how provocative that was.

Probably not. She was as much a dreamer as her cousin Cordelia, though Kate suppressed her desires under countless onionskins of denial. But why play games when she wanted him? Forget the swollen lips. Raised nipples and flushed cheeks told him all he needed to know. And he wanted her. They were two healthy adults with healthy adult appetites, so what was standing in her way?

'I know it sounds ridiculous…'

Wisely, he didn't comment.

She shrugged her shoulders. 'But I have this urge to eat home-made food…'

Urges he understood.

'And to be truthful,' she went on, 'I don't feel it's wise to discuss Caddy's private affairs with waiters hovering at my shoulder. You never know who's listening. The paparazzi have spies everywhere and somewhere noisier and less formal would be safer, in my opinion.'

She talked sense.

'When I flew into Rome I thought I might get the chance to sample some real Italian food,' she went on. 'And this menu…not that I'm not grateful,' she tempered politely, 'is all in French.'

'I see what you mean…' Playing along, he scanned his copy as if he hadn't eaten in the restaurant a thousand times before.

'What do you think?' she pressed.

'I think I know a better place…'

Santino dismissed the chauffeur and took Kate to a place she would never have found without him. It was at the end of a narrow alleyway, and was the sort of noisy café Aunt Meredith had talked about whenever she and Caddy had pressed her for stories from her back-packing youth.

Pushing open a narrow door with no sign over the top of it to hint at what lay behind, Santino invited Kate to go in ahead of him. The noise, heat and aroma of wonderful food hit her full in the face. The small packed space was crammed with tables covered in red gingham tablecloths, and the only light was that provided by candles flickering in wax-caked bottles. Kate started smiling right away. She could hear *'mamma'* shouting instructions from the kitchen, while the red-faced *'papà'* with a tea towel stuck through the ties of his white apron was yelling back to her above the buzz of conversation. Right now their moustachioed host was in the middle of executing an elaborate pirouette as he searched for the correct table upon which to unload the plates and platters wobbling on his outstretched arms.

'I love it,' Kate exclaimed impulsively, 'but can they possibly find space for us?'

The answer came quickly. Having spotted Santino, the chubby restaurateur wiped his hands down the front of his apron and came to welcome them.

'Santino!' Dragging Santino down to his own, much shorter level, the older man kissed him robustly on both cheeks. *'Li vedo portare un ospite!'* he added, pulling back to stare at Kate.

'I see you have brought a visitor.' Santino translated for her briskly. 'For a business meeting,' he informed the older man in English, causing the restaurateur to view Kate speculatively.

'Of course... *Capisco!* I understand,' he cried, instantly adopting a serious expression. 'I hope you're hungry?' he added out of the corner of his mouth for Kate's benefit.

'Starving,' she assured him with a smile.

'Bene...bene!' Rubbing his hands together in anticipation of another hungry customer, their host gazed around until he identified a group about to vacate their table. 'Two minutes, and the table's yours,' he promised Santino with an open-armed flourish.

'Is this all right for you?'

As Santino checked with her Kate thought both his eyes and his voice were daring her to say no. 'This is perfect,' she assured him. 'And once again I apologise for putting you to so much trouble.'

'Please...'

His manner both thrilled and frightened her. As he gave a shrug the inflection in his voice was pure charm, but his eyes were dangerous...there was far too much irony in them.

'You'll have to lose that jacket or melt,' he observed as he shrugged his off. 'Your choice.'

After a moment's hesitation Kate removed her jacket, and

then, because Santino was right about the heat, she opened a couple of buttons at the neck of her shirt too.

They were soon seated in the corner with a mound of fresh crusty bread between them and a bowl of fat green olives slicked with oil. Santino had rolled up his sleeves and the sight of his powerful forearms tanned and shaded with black hair just as Kate remembered them was a worrying distraction. She had to get started on her concerns for Caddy right away and find something safer to think about, she decided.

'That all sounds perfectly reasonable,' Santino agreed after they had discussed everything in detail and agreed safety measures be put in place to prevent anything from upsetting Caddy in the future.

But when the business discussion was over and Kate ran out of things to say she knew it was dangerous to attempt small talk. Who knew where it might lead?

'We can move on to another place,' he suggested after one protracted silence.

Where did he have in mind? There was an air of innocence about him that put Kate immediately on her guard and Santino's eyes were asking questions she didn't want to answer.

Her heart bounced against her chest wall as she considered the possibilities. She should have taken into account the fact that she would be pressed up hard against him in the tiny restaurant. She should have realised they would have to bring their faces very close together in order to hear each other above the noise. 'I'm happy to stay,' she said quickly, sitting back. 'It was a brilliant suggestion. The food is delicious—'

Santino accepted what she said with a faintly ironic smile.

CHAPTER FIVE

THEY sipped vintage cognac with their coffee, warming the honey-coloured liquid in giant-sized glasses they held cupped in their hands. The conversation was flowing more easily now, and Santino confined it strictly to business, for which Kate was relieved. She felt relaxed in his company, which was a first. Until her phone rang…

Glancing at the incoming number, Kate blenched. 'Do you mind if I take this outside?' She was already on her feet.

'No…' Santino's eyes narrowed as she left the table.

After the heat of the café the cool night air was a sharp reminder to Kate of the world she had left behind. 'Meredith?' she said anxiously. 'Is everything all right?'

Aunt Meredith was quick to reassure her that this was just a routine call. She sounded far more concerned about Kate.

'I'm fine!' Kate immediately regretted the force of her claim. She suspected Caddy must have said something to Meredith and Kate knew from experience that Aunt Meredith wasn't easy to fool. 'Everything's going really well…' But by the time the call was finished Kate knew she hadn't convinced Meredith, who knew her better than her own mother had ever done.

'Sorry about that,' Kate said as she joined Santino at the

table. She felt a flutter of concern when she noticed that her coffee-cup had been refilled. It appeared as if Santino was in no hurry to bring the evening to a close.

'Not a problem for me… And not a problem for you, I hope?' His gaze was keen as he searched her face.

'No.' Kate laughed it off, but inside she was aching with guilty secrets. There were too many of them locked inside her, of which her daughter was just one. And now here she was, sitting with Francesca's father. It seemed incredible, and it frightened Kate to think that Santino didn't even know of Francesca's existence.

And nor could he until she was sure of him.

'You seemed concerned when you identified the number,' he probed casually.

He wasn't going to let it go, Kate realised. 'It was Aunt Meredith, Caddy's mother, ringing to check that everything is all right. You can understand her concerns for Caddy…'

She could tell Santino wasn't convinced by her glib excuses. She had set alarm bells ringing, which was the last thing she had wanted to do. 'So…?' To avoid looking at him she began gathering her things together, hoping that Santino would take the hint and suggest the time had come for them to leave.

'So…' He mimicked her ironically, viewing her over the rim of his coffee-cup as if they were hours away from bringing the evening to a close. 'Why don't you tell me something about yourself, Kate?'

Kate was sure her heart stopped beating. 'Like what?'

Such as why she was doing a good impression of a hedgehog curling into a defensive ball might be a start, Santino reflected. 'How you first came to be interested in the film industry?' He was prepared to take everything one step at a time if that was what it took. They had covered Kate's concerns for Caddy and they had established that the connection between them was as strong as ever. Now it was time for the interview for the position he had in mind…

'Working in the film industry wasn't my idea to begin with,' she admitted. 'It was Meredith's—'

'Meredith's? What did your parents think of that?'

He could see her thought processes clicking into the appropriate grooves. She was deciding whether or not to trust him with some small detail from her life…weighing up whether it would be worth it to distract him from some bigger issues, perhaps?

'They were never part of the equation.'

'I see…' He didn't, of course, but he didn't want to knock her off track. She made it easy for him when she began speaking again without prompting.

'I wasn't sure what I wanted to do when I left school and Meredith had contacts in the film industry. She gave me the introduction I needed, and I thought, Why not? I wasn't too keen at first, but I grew into it.'

As her face lit up he suggested, 'And came to love it in the end?'

'That's right.' She looked at him as if she hadn't thought he would be interested in what she found good about her life, but his tactic had always been to find out what people wanted and then to give it to them. It was so simple he found it hard to understand why everyone hadn't found the same route to success. 'From what I've seen there's no doubt you have a way with people…' He dealt her the compliment that he knew would boost her confidence, bringing him another step closer to his goal.

'Thank you.'

Her eyes softened to a misty grey as she looked at him and he could tell that his words were having the desired effect.

They were both trying to fathom out what each of them wanted from the other. But now something else had crept into her eyes…was it wariness, or something more? If he hadn't known better he might have thought it a sign that he had hurt her in some way. But he had never left a string of broken hearts in his wake. He only ever dealt in adult relationships with women who knew their own mind, women just like Kate…

To reassure himself he took his mind back to the night when she had raked him with her fingernails and begged him not to stop, never to stop… It was hard for a man to forget a thing like that, impossible for him to forget a woman like Kate, unthinkable that he would let her get away a second time. 'I'd like to make you an offer…'

When she looked at him keenly he knew the moment had come to close the deal. 'I'd like you to stay on here in Rome and work for me.'

'Work for you?' She was clearly incredulous.

'What's wrong with that?' He was growing impatient. No one had ever refused the offer of a job in his organisation.

'I can't, that's all—'

'You can't?' he cut across her. 'Or you won't?'

'I'm sorry, Santino, I really can't… Couldn't you get someone else?'

'I want you.' His jaw firmed.

'You…'

Even as the light of hope sparked in her eyes her voice faded in recognition of her mistake. She knew Santino Rossi would never want her the way she wanted him. He felt a rush of triumph as he interpreted the signs. Kate was a good actress, but not that good. She might act prim, but there were fires burning very close to the surface of this new Kate Mulhoon's decorous manner.

'I'm only offering you a job, Kate…'

She flinched at the put-down, but quickly recovered.

'I already have a job…two jobs, in fact. I represent Caddy at the agency, and for the time being at least I'm her manager. Obviously there's a conflict of interest and I won't—'

'Remain her manager? Stay at the agency? Well, now you won't have to because I'm offering you a job.'

'Look, all of this is so sudden…'

And the last thing she wanted was to antagonise him with a flat refusal, he guessed. He let her squirm for a while.

'I don't know what to say,' she said at last, clearly thrown.

'You don't have to say anything right away. Think about it. You've got until tomorrow morning to decide.' He liked deadlines. When he put one in place something had to happen. Inactivity killed him.

'Why me, Santino?' She looked at him curiously.

Because the window of opportunity was open and he had never been one to walk on by. 'Because after this debacle on the set I know I need to hire someone who understands the business, someone who works well with my team, which you've already proved you can do, someone who can liaise between me and my people on the ground. It would be a vast improvement on your present position back in London. You'd have your own department. You'd report directly to me—'

'This is all going way too fast—'

'Really?' He angled his head to stare at her. 'I've never had the impression that you're slow…'

No response.

'My organisation needs someone like you.' He threw her a smile. 'Just think about it…'

'You don't hold back, do you?' she whispered, fixed on his gaze.

'Salary wouldn't be a problem—'

'No… Sorry…I can't stay on in Rome.'

Her voice was flat as if reality had kicked in, extinguishing the fantasy he had spun for her. He was disappointed, of course. But defeat wasn't in his lexicon and he wasn't about to back off now.

'I have to be back in the UK by this weekend at the latest,' she went on, voicing some inner thought and unwittingly handing him a compromise.

'Okay…' He eased his shoulders in a shrug as if it didn't matter to him one way or the other what she did, but his mind was scrutinising the facts—she was an intelligent woman, and he had just given her the opportunity of a lifetime. There had to be something else. Someone else? Was this feeling jealousy? If so, it had to be a first. He kept his face impassive as he delved a little deeper. 'Of course, if you have personal reasons—'

'I don't. At least…'

'Go on.' He could hardly hold back the bite in his voice.

She clammed up. She retreated into herself leaving only the prickles on show. He eased off too. Like all good negotiators, he knew when to take his foot off the gas. 'Well, if you could just stay until the weekend, by which time the new director should have settled in, I'd appreciate it. And of course I'd pay you well for your time…'

Nothing.

He tried again. 'I'm sure Cordelia would appreciate the reassurance of having you around during the changeover of directors…'

Bullseye.

'You won't have to pay me,' she assured him tightly. 'I'll happily stay on until the weekend if it reassures Cordelia.

My cousin's a wonderful actress. You don't know how lucky you are…'

And neither did cousin Cordelia, Santino thought, dropping his gaze to hide his rush of triumph.

CHAPTER SIX

BY THE time Santino had signed the bill Kate was already regretting her decision to stay on in Rome. Giving Caddy the boost she needed to regain her confidence was one thing, but she could have remained at Caddy's side without agreeing to work for Santino, and reporting directly to him was madness. What had she been thinking?

'Ready?'

As Santino stood up and prepared to hold her chair Kate was forced to accept that she could never think clearly when Santino was involved. And it certainly didn't help now when a lock of inky-black hair caught on his lashes as he looked at her. But she had to remain detached. It was either that, or break her silence and face a lifetime of regret.

'Kate?'

'Sorry...' Kate grabbed her jacket, evading Santino's attempts to help her to put it on. Buttoning it up securely, she didn't forget the buttons at the neck of her shirt were open and fastened those too.

As Santino watched Kate fastening up her suit and her blouse, sealing the package up tight, he felt suspicion grind inside him. There had to be someone else back home. This act was too contrived. A woman didn't turn from seductress to celibate in the space of five years with all her allure intact. Kate had all the hallmarks of a tease. It warned him to be wary and question rather than trust. But for some reason he wanted Kate; he wanted her to be different from other women.

But he only had to examine the facts to know he couldn't afford to let her in. Five years ago he had taken what she'd freely offered, no meaningless pledges on either side. There had been no time for anything other than feeling and hunger. She had responded wholeheartedly, but afterwards he had felt emptier than before. He had known then he was yearning for something he could never have.

'*Arrivederci*, Santino!'

'*Arrivederci*, Federico!' The distraction of the ebullient restaurateur's farewell came as a relief. This was no time to be dwelling on the past.

'Goodbye, Federico…'

Kate turned and waved. She seemed harmless enough. Or was that an act too? Was she like every other woman—out for what she could get? Was she painting herself in a rosy light so everyone would love her and let their guard down? She had begun by opening up and telling him about her life with Cordelia and Meredith, and then for no reason she had clammed up again. Why? It couldn't be second thoughts about the job, or fear of the responsibility she had agreed to take on—she could eat the job. Which left the phone call. Who was waiting for Kate back home aside from Aunt Meredith? He needed more time with her to find out what was going on. He would much rather stick salt in the wound now and prove her treachery than continue to pursue her wearing a blindfold.

'I thought we'd walk back to the Russie, cool off after the heat in the restaurant,' he suggested. 'Do you mind?' He held the door for her, closing his eyes as she passed to better appreciate her light crushed-petal scent.

'No, that would be great,' she said. 'I like to walk...'

He could tell she had relaxed a little. She even granted him a small smile as she tilted up her face to look at him. But then he remembered how professional she was about everything now; she was always on her guard.

'I've had a wonderful evening, Santino, and I want to thank you for indulging me. I know it was a business meeting and I had no right to drag you off to a place of my choice, but Federico's restaurant was everything I hoped to find when I came to Rome.'

She knew just what to say to make a good impression on him. But how much of it was contrived to make him soften towards her? 'It was my pleasure.' As always he hid his true feelings behind a mask of good manners. 'I'm so glad you enjoyed yourself.'

'Is it far to the Russie from here?' She looked up and down the narrow street as she spoke to him.

'No.' His brow creased as his mind whirled with possibilities for the rest of the evening.

'Then why don't you leave me here and I'll walk the rest of the way?'

'You'll do no such thing.' He hadn't expected that. He was rattled. Her independence irritated him. He wasn't used to women striking out on their own—not when he was around. He made the decisions. 'I can't let you walk through the streets of Rome on your own at night.'

'Then I'll take a cab.'

'You can't just flag one down.'

'A bus, then.'

Incredibly, before he knew what she was doing she had

nimbly sidestepped him and hopped onto the running board of one of the buses that made up the city's sightseeing service.

'What do you think you're doing?' He had no option but to jump on after her.

'Being spontaneous. Going on a bus tour…' There was a look of determination on her face as she fished in her purse for the fare.

'Go upstairs. Grab the front seats and I'll pay…' He couldn't believe he was saying it—couldn't believe he was travelling on a bus.

He slid in beside her. She had managed to secure one of the prized seats at the front and was fiddling with the headphones connected to the translation service. She blinked when he twitched the speakers from her ears.

'Don't you trust me to be your guide? I am a Roman…'

'As if there could be any doubt,' she told him as the bus chugged closer to the floodlit Colosseum.

It was the closest she'd come to flirting with him. That thought soothed his wounded pride and filled him with another sort of emotion altogether. Which was somewhat short-lived, because now her face was deadpan again.

It was a long time since he'd had to think about his city's history, but for Kate he'd make the effort. He settled down and pointed towards one of the yawning gaps in the ancient walls. 'Can you see the arena down there?'

She shuddered involuntarily. He didn't blame her. Parts of the ancient building were practically intact. All that was missing was the roar of the bloodthirsty crowd.

She shivered again.

'Are you cold?'

'No, I'm fine,' she lied. There was a chilly breeze and so he shrugged off his jacket.

'No, thank you, I'm warm enough,' she lied again, seeing what he was about to do.

'You're only wearing a lightweight suit,' he pointed out, draping the jacket round her shoulders.

'And what about you?'

He wasn't aware of anything other than the need to take care of her and that was dangerous. 'I can't have you catching cold after a night out with the boss.' He kept it impersonal. Time to give them both a reminder that this bus trip was only a rather unusual sidebar to a business meeting.

'Are you worried I'll be late in tomorrow?' Both her voice and her grey eyes surprised him by turning warm with amusement and his lips tugged with pleasure at the thought that she was going to be working for him—for a few days at least. He couldn't remember feeling this way about work, or about a woman, ever.

As they passed another ancient ruin she reached for her headphones. 'You're supposed to be my tour guide,' she reminded him as she started to untangle them.

'And so I am…' He gently prised them from her fingers. And had to fight the urge to hold onto her hands a little longer.

'We're passing the Temple of Vesta,' he informed her to break the sudden tension. He put the headphones on the seat between them, easing away to put some space between them. Did she ever think about that night? And how was he supposed to remember his history with that sort of erotic distraction playing on his mind?

He kept it short. Rome was so closely packed with antiquities they'd be on to the next one if he didn't keep it brief. 'The temple was a cruel place. Girls as young as six were chosen from some of the best families in Rome and taken to live at the temple. Their young lives were stolen from them—'

Kate's heart contracted as Santino started to explain the ancient traditions and her mouth had turned completely dry by the time she managed to force out, 'Really?'

Thankfully Santino didn't appear to notice her sudden change of attitude.

'The Vestal Virgins were selected for their beauty…' He paused as she turned to look at him.

'Go on, don't stop,' Kate prompted.

There was a time when she had said those words to him under very different circumstances and it was hard for him to concentrate on the history lesson when her fragrant breath was sweeping his mouth. He had to stop himself staring at her lips. 'The Vestals' task was to keep the fire burning inside the temple.' As her fire had burned inside him for five long years. 'Each of them spent ten years in training, ten years as Vestals and ten years training novices before they were allowed to leave the temple. Then they could get married—'

'And live happily every after?'

'Irony, Kate?'

As if she had just realised there was a very small space between them she pulled back, and he turned away. In his head the bitter side of life had overtaken the sweet, exposing it for what it was—a panacea, a lure, a chimera, a deception. 'The life of a Vestal wasn't without risk.' His voice hardened. It was as if he had to spoil it for her. 'If one of them broke her vow of chastity she was buried alive in Campo Scellerato, the Field of Villains, and her lover was flogged to death in the Forum.'

'That's horrible.'

'That's Roman history. You can't hold me directly responsible.'

'I think I know that, Santino.'

Her cheeks were flushed, but she held his gaze. The fact that she stood up to him was a novelty and gave him a charge.

'I can't believe people could be so cruel.'

'Oh, they can, believe me.' He held her gaze long enough to get a reaction and was curious when it slid away as if she was hiding something from him. They sat in silence for quite a while after that and then she surprised him by touching his arm.

'You look sad,' she said. 'Is something wrong?'

'Sad?' Disappointed yet again by a woman, perhaps. He shrugged it off. 'Momentary lapse.' But when he stared into her eyes this time he noticed how her glance wandered to his lips. They were so close together their lips were almost touching. Instead of pulling away she remained quite still. *She expected him to kiss her.* She wanted him to kiss her. But he would choose the time, not Kate.

His rebuff made her tense and withdrawn, and she didn't sit still again after that.

'How far is it to the Hotel Russie now?' she said as the bus turned a corner.

She was already restless as it slowed in preparation to take on board another group of tourists and he could tell she was itching to get off. 'We can walk there in about ten minutes from here, if that's what you want to do?'

'Yes, please. I do…'

She was already up and waiting for him to get out of her way so she could make good her escape. He stood and let her go past him in the narrow aisle and then she hurried down the steps. The moment they stepped onto the pavement she was looking up and down the street as if trying to orientate herself.

'Which way is it?' she murmured, half to herself.

'I'll take you.' But she didn't even hear him. She was off like a hare from the trap and when he caught up with her he had to point out she was going the wrong way. She turned without comment and he had to swing into a brisk walk to keep up with her.

But there was only so much dogged independence he could take. He let her get ahead, and when she finally realised he wasn't there any more and stopped to look for him he held up his hands, palms flat. 'I don't know what's got into you, Kate. I only hope it doesn't get in the way of your work.'

'I haven't let anyone down yet,' she assured him, keeping her eyes fixed on her goal—which was the Russie.

'Don't make this a first,' he warned. 'When I hire the best I expect top class results.'

'You'll get them.' She walked faster. 'I've no intention of letting you down.'

'Good,' he said, striding casually along by her side. 'Just checking.'

It would have suited Kate at that moment to bury her head beneath the pillows at the hotel and forget the evening with Santino had ever happened. It was agony wanting Santino to like her when that made her so weak. *Like her?* She was kidding herself; she wanted him to want her.

So much for their dinner date being nothing more than a business meeting! If she could be honest with herself for just a moment she would be forced to admit that for her it had been so much more. She had wanted him to kiss her. She had wanted to let her defences down. That was how dangerous Santino was. And he had played her like a master. She couldn't get away from him fast enough now, and turned the instant they reached the hotel entrance.

'Goodnight, Santino, and thank you again for a lovely evening.'

He ignored the hint, and, leaning across, opened the door

for her before the doorman had a chance, and then he stepped inside and insisted on escorting her to the lift.

As they waited for the elevator Santino felt as if the volcano Kate had been stepping around all night was ready to blow. She had agreed to give him a few days of her time, nothing more. It was an insult to his pride.

She had wanted him to kiss her, and was still smarting from the fact that he hadn't. But he wouldn't allow himself to be lured into a honey trap by a woman he suspected of deception. Whatever happened between them would be on his terms. Whatever she was hiding he would find out. Until then it pleased him to observe and bide his time.

It was on occasions like this he realised that his childhood had imbued him with certain advantages. The sudden departure of his mother and death of his father had forced him to learn how to survive on his wits. He had become unusually perceptive, which accounted for his meteoric rise in the world of business. That and the fact that he'd had nowhere to go but up.

He wasn't about to throw everything away on a woman—even if that woman was Kate Mulhoon. He was always alert to the possibility of scandal, or a trap, and Kate was condemned by her own hand. She had been quite prepared to kiss him when there was clearly someone waiting for her back home. *And if she had considered betraying that individual, why not him?*

'Santino—'

'Yes?' He was standing in the shadows where his thoughts were unreadable, whereas Kate was in a pool of light cast by one of the elaborate chandeliers. It gave him chance to examine her face. She was beautiful in an unaffected way. And he wanted to believe that her beauty was more than skin deep, but past experience warned him that was unlikely.

The lift bell rang and the doors slid open, which was a cue for her to hold out her hand in the formal manner for him to shake.

'Thank you again, Santino,' she said coolly.

At first he was affronted by her composure; her voice so detached and aloof. For a moment he thought he might have read her wrong, but when he brought her hand to his lips he felt her tremble.

CHAPTER SEVEN

KATE was glad Caddy had decided not to wait up for her. She didn't want to relive every moment of an evening that had left her so confused. In order not to disturb her cousin she closed the door carefully, with a barely discernible click.

There were so many shadows in her past and so many secrets she could hardly bring herself to face, let alone confide them to Santino, and none of this was easy to share. How could she admit to Caddy that she had wanted Santino to kiss her and that he almost had, but for some reason had pulled back? How could she admit how disappointed she had been? Santino knew she wanted him, and his response had been to reject her; she couldn't be more humiliated.

But at least the business side of things had gone well. She had been given all the assurances she had asked for regarding Caddy's position. So at least there was nothing wrong with her business acumen even if her judgement when it came to her personal life remained severely flawed.

She knew she had to tell Santino that he was Francesca's father. But the longer she left it, the harder it would be. She still wanted to know more about him before she could trust him with Francesca's future. She could only hope that working alongside him would give her that opportunity—

'Kate? Is that you?'

Kate's breath caught in her throat as Caddy's sleepy voice reached her from the bedroom.

'Yes, it's me… I'm sorry I woke you—'

'Did you tell him? Did you tell Santino about Francesca?'

It was Caddy's first thought too. Of course it was.

'We'll talk about it tomorrow. Go back to sleep now, Caddy. You're due back on the lot in just a few hours…'

The next morning Kate was relieved when Caddy didn't mention their brief conversation in the middle of the night. But she knew Caddy suspected something was up, and the name Santino Rossi hung in the air between them like an unspoken threat.

'Where's my suit?' Kate asked when they were both getting dressed. 'I'm sure I left it in the bedroom, and now it's gone.'

Caddy's gaze slid away.

'Where is it, Caddy?' Kate pressed, her suspicions growing. Half of her was glad they could be discussing mundane things like what to wear, while the other half of her was on the point of panic. She didn't need things going wrong in the one part of her life she could usually rely on to provide her with an anchor. Work had been her saviour on so many occasions, allowing her to immerse herself in a world that left her with little time to dwell on the past.

'When I saw it hanging over the chair I thought you must have left it out for cleaning,' Caddy said, reclaiming Kate's attention. 'I sent them both to the laundry, just to be on the safe side—'

'Both my suits?' Kate exploded, knowing she was over-reacting for reasons she couldn't explore now. 'What am I supposed to wear to work?'

'Calm down,' Caddy said, putting an arm around her shoulder. 'You're going to wear something fabulous from my wardrobe—'

'I'm going to work, not a première,' Kate pointed out, raking her hair with exasperation.

'Thanks for reminding me about your hair,' Caddy said, refusing to be dismayed. 'You know, you should have highlights—'

'Not a chance.' Kate was already scraping her hair back as a prelude to tying it securely out of the way.

'A trim, then?'

'I'm happy with my hair the way it is. What's Santino going to think if I turn up for my first day at work with a new haircut and wearing your paint-me-on jeans?'

'So, do you care what Santino thinks?'

Yes, she did, and that was the trouble.

'Perhaps you're right about the jeans,' Caddy admitted thoughtfully.

'I know I am. Look, you'd better call Housekeeping and see if they can return my suits—'

Caddy's response was to walk across the room and delve into her collection of exclusive carrier bags. With a cry of triumph she plucked out a dress made from the softest cashmere. In a wonderful soft buttery gold colour, it was a simple tube of a dress with nothing that Kate could take exception to. The sleeves were long and slightly bell-shaped and the length was respectable. The neck was high and slashed, showing some flesh, but nothing too revealing.

'It's absolutely gorgeous, but not for me,' Kate said firmly. 'And you haven't even worn it yet,' she added.

'It's no big deal if you borrow it for one day. And as you've got nothing else to wear…'

She was in a corner, and Caddy knew it. The hotel had proved to be so efficient in every way Kate couldn't imagine the laundry service would let it down. Her suits wouldn't be returned for another twenty-four hours and she had to wear something…

'And don't forget these,' Caddy insisted.

'No,' Kate said flatly. Caddy's enthusiasm had to be curbed somehow. She was holding out a pair of fabulous cream suede boots. Close fitting to the knee with a medium-height heel, they laced up the side and were finished with a buckle. The brand name on the box was enough to tell Kate they had cost a small fortune.

'Why not?' Caddy shook them provocatively.

'They're so delicate. I might spoil them.'

'You?' Caddy huffed with amusement. 'I don't think so, Kate.'

'But my own shoes are in the bedroom. I'll go and get them—'

Caddy cut her off at the door. 'If you think for one moment I'm going to allow you to wear those flat boots with my divine new dress you are absolutely wrong, Kate Mulhoon. You're my manager, remember? You've got to dress the part now.'

Kate frowned as Caddy retreated into the bedroom leaving the tempting articles behind her. She had been outmanoeuvred for once.

Dressing quickly, Kate glanced at her watch. It was still too early to call Francesca, which she badly wanted to do. She called for a cab instead to take Caddy and herself to the studio. She'd call home later, the first chance she got…

The moment she put the phone down Kate overheard Caddy chatting away to Meredith on her mobile. She couldn't hear the words, only that Caddy sounded concerned and then excited…

She shouldn't be listening, Kate told herself firmly, collecting up her things. Meredith was Caddy's mother, and they were entitled to a private conversation.

'Caddy, come on,' Kate called the moment she heard Caddy walking across the room. 'The cab rank's only across the street and the taxi driver will be waiting for us. We don't want to be late…'

Kate had some free time on her hands when she arrived at the film studios. While Caddy was in Make-up she took the bull by the horns and had her hair trimmed. She felt a little unsure at first about the new modern style, but the hairdresser soon reassured her, and Kate had to admit she was quite pleased with her new look.

'Why don't you let Marie have a go at your face next?' Caddy suggested after approving the finished result.

'It's that bad?' Kate grinned.

'Worse.' Caddy laughed as she pulled a mock grimace.

By the time Kate walked onto the set she was transformed. Wearing the smart outfit, and with her hair trimmed into a face-framing bob, she was attracting more attention than she had ever done. It felt strange to begin with, but then it felt great. She felt great. Until the moment Santino appeared on set and strode straight up to her.

'What on earth have you done to your hair?'

His obvious disapproval shocked Kate and stabbed into her newfound self-esteem. But the last thing she intended was for Santino to know how she felt. She tipped her chin and referred him to her clipboard, angling it in front of him so he had nowhere else to look. 'I wasn't aware that the job required me to adopt a particular hairstyle.'

As he stared at her she held his gaze until it was Santino who looked away. Then she made a point of saying, 'Good morning, Santino.' She said it brightly, determined he wasn't going to have everything his own way. 'There are a few things we need to go over—'

'Such as?' He looked her up and down.

'The showers ran out of hot water yesterday,' Kate continued briskly, 'and the on-set catering needs an urgent review. The toast was burnt today and there weren't enough eggs to go round—'

'Really?' Santino murmured.

The expression in his eyes made Kate's heart thump painfully in her chest and she had to force herself to concentrate. 'Yes, and that's not all—'

'It is for now.' Taking her by the arm, Santino steered her out of earshot of everyone else on the set. 'I tried to ring to tell you what I planned for today, but both the hotel phone and Cordelia's mobile were engaged. You'll have to give me your mobile number, Kate. I expect to get hold of you whenever I need you even if you are only working for me for a few days.'

Kate ground her jaw and somehow managed to remain silent. It was clear she should have read the small print before agreeing to work for Santino. It appeared he demanded twenty-four-hour availability as well as an approved hairstyle.

'If I could have got hold of either of you it would have saved Cordelia the trouble of arriving on the set so early,' he went on. 'What on earth was so important both of you were on your phones so early in the morning?'

'I can't speak for Cordelia—' Kate's pleasant tone belied the anger rising inside her '—but I was ringing for a taxi to bring us here.' She wasn't about to be intimidated.

'There's no point in Cordelia hanging around the set without a director to direct. You should have known that, Kate. Tell her she can go—'

Kate's first thought was, *Tell her yourself!* But a show of emotion wasn't appropriate between employee and employer. She had worked for difficult people in the past and knew how to handle them. And no one had forced her into this job. She had agreed to take on the role of Santino's PA for a few days until he hired a proper assistant, because it suited her—on a number of levels, not least of which was making sure Cordelia's best interests were always at the forefront of Santino's mind.

'I imagine your client will appreciate having the time to perfect her role.'

'I'm sure she will, and thank you for your consideration,' Kate said coolly. This wasn't about her, or how she felt about Santino, this was about Caddy and work, and... *If only life could be that simple!* Right now she was trying not to breathe in case she inhaled Santino's intoxicating cologne and was willing her body not to tingle all over just because he was within touching distance.

'You'd better come with me—' his voice was brusque, his glance impatient '—and I'll go over what's expected of you.'

Accustomed as she was to difficult people, Kate had to take several deep breaths before she could trust herself to speak. 'Good idea,' she managed pleasantly.

'We'll talk over breakfast.'

'Breakfast?' Another meal together? Another opportunity to sit close to Santino? Another opportunity to have her mind blanked and her senses take her over?

'A breakfast meeting suits me.'

'I'm sure it does,' Kate murmured under her breath as she followed him. Any excuse to exert his authority over her suited Santino. 'Do we have time for breakfast?'

He stopped, and after a moment turned. The tug of self-assurance at one corner of his mouth made her heart thunder.

'I'm the boss, Kate. If I say we've got time, we've got time.'

He hid it well, but he was still smarting as he watched her rush off to tell Cordelia where she was going. He couldn't accept Kate had someone back in England and wouldn't admit as much to him. He had hired her because she was happy to take the heat, but who took the heat for her? Jealousy ripped through him at the thought that there was someone back in the UK who did that for her, someone she was eager to get back to by the weekend.

But jealousy was disabling and not an emotion that Santino was used to.

'You mentioned breakfast?' she reminded him calmly when she returned.

She was prompting him? And she was acting as if there were nothing between them—no sexual tension, no undercurrents, no unanswered questions. She didn't appear to be rattled in the slightest. Far from it, her face was composed as if she was resigned to dealing with truculent employers.

'We need to talk,' he said bluntly, dipping his head to stare into her eyes.

'Talk about what? The job?'

There it was again…anxiety in her gaze. Then she looked away, proving he was right to be suspicious. She was just as untrustworthy as the rest of her sex. He would keep the pressure on until she told him everything.

'You can leave your clipboard here; you won't be needing it.' He could sense her unease growing. She knew breakfast gave him another chance to probe.

'I'll get my bag.'

'You do that.' He watched her walk away. He had to admit she looked fantastic. She could have given any starlet a run for her money. The soft suede boots drew his attention to the length of her legs, and the slim column of a dress clung to her hips, moulding them as she moved. If she strolled along the Via Veneto dressed like that she would stop the traffic. Did she have any idea how sexy she looked?

Almost certainly. She had all the grace of a feline predator wedded to the prim characteristics of a Victorian maid—an explosive combination. She had a new haircut and the outfit suited her. Was she trying to impress him? If so she had succeeded. Like a costume she might have put on to play a role in one of his films, the elegant outfit had affected the way she walked and even the way she felt about herself, he guessed. She oozed confidence, which was a very attractive quality in a woman. But he was sick of women thinking all they had to do was lie on their back to hit the jackpot. A night with him wasn't a passport to riches, it was a journey to nowhere.

When she got back she reminded him the canteen wasn't open yet.

If she thought he was going to call off breakfast she was wrong. 'Looks like we'll have to eat somewhere else.' He shrugged, having never intended to eat at the studio. 'I'll go and get the car and pick you up at the gate in five minutes.'

Her grip tightened on her bag, but she kept the panic under control.

'Where will we go?' she called after him.

'Somewhere typical of the region.' He couldn't resist it, and was smiling when he started walking away.

'Not too far away, I hope. I've got a lot of work to do.'

His jaw firmed. He admired her grit, but he wasn't prepared to give an inch. 'Not too far away.' He glanced in the direction of the hills above Rome. He was allowed a small lie, wasn't he?

* * *

Kate's heart sank as Santino's sleek black Maserati drew up outside the hotel. He had brought her to the hills above Rome, and it had taken hours. Thanks to the heavy traffic they had travelled the whole way at a crawl. She would be lucky to be back at the studio before it closed for the day, and she had wanted to review the ordering procedures in the canteen.

'Ready?' Santino said to her as he passed his keys through the car window to the hotel valet.

'You're the boss,' she reminded him with faint sarcasm.

And didn't he like her to know it? Kate thought as Santino came around the front of the vehicle to open the door for her. Climbing out, she stared up at the impressive façade of the pale sandstone building.

'Does it meet with your approval?' Santino enquired without the slightest interest in her reply, Kate suspected, well aware of the irony.

But the truth was, the hotel was magnificent. It was the hotel equivalent of the first restaurant he had taken her to, but this time she kept her thoughts to herself. For one thing, they had driven for miles without seeing a single habitation, so she could hardly ask if they could go somewhere else!

'I've brought you here for a reason,' Santino explained, giving nothing away as he steered her towards the revolving doors.

Kate's heart fluttered with anxiety. However many times she tried to reassure herself that this was only a business meeting, she couldn't help wondering what Santino really had in mind…and why he had brought her to such a magnificent place so far away from the film studio.

He wanted to test her to the full. He was going to ask the questions any boss should ask of his employee—marital status, for one.

As they approached the entrance the doors swung open and

the bellboy and hotel manager appeared at once as if some internal grapevine had alerted them.

'Signor Rossi.' The manager inclined his head with respect. 'We are delighted to welcome you and your guest. What can I do for you?'

'I realise La Pergola is closed for lunch, but—'

'Closed? Not for you, Signor Rossi.'

'I was hoping you would say that, Fritz. Ms Mulhoon is over here from England.'

'I will alert the chef.'

He held up a restraining hand. 'There's no need for that. A light snack is all we require. We have some business to talk over.'

The manager bowed. 'I understand.'

He curbed his smile. He doubted it, though to 'understand' and be discreet was any successful hotelier's rule of thumb. 'I would like to show Ms Mulhoon the view.'

'Of course, Signor Rossi. Ah, the view…' It was Kate's turn to receive a bow. 'In the words of your own Charles Dickens, "Here was Rome indeed at last; and such a Rome as no one can imagine in its full and awful grandeur…"'

'Like the Colosseum…' Kate smiled and then grimaced when she thought no one was looking. Santino thought he saw a prescient shiver run across her shoulders, which only added fuel to his suspicions. What did she have to be apprehensive about here at such a lovely hotel, if not his questions?

'I'm eager to see the view,' she said, quickly recovering as she turned to smile at the hotel manager. Santino suspected she was relieved to have someone else walking with them.

Having led them across the lobby and along a discreetly lit corridor the hotel manager threw open some heavy double doors with a flourish. 'Please…' he invited, standing aside to allow Kate to pass.

'Quite something, isn't it?' Santino murmured. He was already anticipating Kate's reaction.

She stood quite still for a moment and then turned to look at him. 'It's breathtaking…' She was smiling in amazement.

He guessed the view so surpassed her expectations she had forgotten the tensions that existed between them for a moment.

'I've never seen anything like it before.' She turned back to look.

The whole of Rome was spread out in front of them, with St Peter's dome prominently in view.

'I can't take it in…'

She was breathless and the way she clutched her chest drew his gaze. 'I'm glad you approve.'

'Won't you sit down?' Fritz invited, smiling as he led the way to some tables by the window. 'I'll have the chef prepare some small snack… Carpaccio of scampi on a lime gelée with papaya, caviar and tequila ice crush, perhaps? Or some tagliolini with broccoli and clams…?'

Kate had to resist the temptation to ask if it was possible to have a cheese sandwich.

'Three Michelin stars,' Santino whispered discreetly, just in time. But as his warm breath swept her neck every tiny hair on the back of her neck stood to attention. 'Could we have something light?' She was glad of the distraction and smiled up at Fritz. 'It all sounds delicious, but—'

'I understand.' The hotel manager beamed. 'May I suggest pigeon breast on warm oranges with mulled wine sauce followed by a selection of cheeses from the trolley?'

'Just the selection of cheeses from the trolley would be fine for me,' Kate assured him.

'And for me too,' Santino said. 'We don't want to put the chef to any trouble. I'm sure he must be fully occupied preparing for tonight's guests…'

Was this sudden show of consideration for her benefit? Kate wondered.

Even though he had failed to tempt them the manager scarcely missed a beat. 'Would you care to see the wine list, Signor Rossi?'

'Thank you, no. We'll have a glass of champagne and a bottle of San Pellegrino sparkling water.'

'Certainly.'

Franz bowed his way out of their company with a smile as warm and as genuine as if they had ordered up the most expensive items on the menu. But as he disappeared Kate grew increasingly tense when Santino seemed in no hurry to start the conversation. He was waiting for her to say something…to give something away, perhaps?

'Nice man,' Santino commented at last, settling back in his chair. 'Don't you think so, Kate?'

Kate knew that was only his opening gambit. Santino hadn't brought her here to admire the scenery. 'Very nice,' she agreed, having decided to confine herself to simple answers. She wished she were a million miles away. She wished she could lose the urge to stare at Santino…

'In the summer you can eat out on the terrace overlooking the whole of Rome. It's quite magnificent.'

'Really?' Kate murmured distractedly. 'I'm sorry I won't be here to see it…' All the thoughts whirling through her head were making her careless.

CHAPTER EIGHT

OF COURSE it wasn't just cheese and biscuits from a super-market shelf; the waiters brought them fresh crunchy bread, succulent green olives, and a selection of fine cheeses that would have put Paxton & Whitfield, the great London cheese shop, to shame.

Kate had to keep reminding herself to remain guarded when Santino began to share some behind-the-scenes facts with her, allowing her a brief glimpse of the man beneath the driven entrepreneur. In spite of all her self-imposed warnings she was starting to relax, even starting to like him, but that didn't mean she judged it the right time to tell him about Francesca. She needed a lot more reassurance before she could bring herself to do that.

'So, tell me about your life in England...'

She should have known, Kate realised. Santino hadn't risen to the top of the tree without good reason. This was how he nailed a deal...he softened up the opposition before going in for the kill. But she was ready for him. 'As you know, I work at the agency that handles Caddy—'

'Worked, past tense, if I had my way. Go on.'

'I use a small apartment in town on the odd occasions when I'm forced to work late.'

'And when you're not working late?'

She really had his attention now, Kate thought as Santino leaned towards her. 'I live with Aunt Meredith and Caddy in the country—when Caddy's there, of course.' She thought he looked pleased by her answer, and maybe a little more than that. Her heart raced furiously as he stared at her.

'You live with Cordelia and her mother?' Santino's dark eyes were probing her deepest thoughts, warning Kate to take care with her answer.

'Yes, I do.'

'So what's your marital status?'

'What's yours?' she flung back at him, totally thrown.

'That's a very personal question.' Santino held her gaze.

'And yours wasn't?'

'My question was directed at a prospective employee.'

Kate's cheeks fired up with embarrassment. She had walked straight into the trap Santino had laid for her. 'I'm single and happy to remain so.'

'Defensive too.'

'Not at all; I'm just happy the way I am. My life is full. I don't need a man to define me—'

She was just getting into her stride when Santino's phone rang.

'Will you excuse me?' He was already on his feet, frowning at the interruption.

'Go right ahead.' Kate could hardly hide her relief as Santino walked away. She was keen to learn more about him, but when the tables were turned her mouth ran away with her. She didn't want to lie to him, but she was nowhere near ready to tell him the truth…any of it.

Santino was smiling when he returned to the table.

'Good news?' Kate was beginning to hope he had been

called away. She needed some time alone to review her tactics if she wasn't going to make a mess of telling him about Francesca.

'I think it's good news,' he said, 'and I hope you agree. Our new director has arrived ahead of schedule.'

'But that's excellent news.' And the best reason yet to put the distance she needed to think clearly between them. Kate started to her feet. 'We should get back.'

'You're in a hurry to leave.'

There was a warning note in Santino's voice, which warned Kate to relax. She made a point of settling back in her chair. 'Not at all, I just thought—'

'We're not going back to the studio,' Santino cut across her. 'There's a little restaurant higher up the valley where it's become a tradition for the studio to hold a welcome party at the start of each new project.'

'And with a new director starting it's a new project.'

'Exactly.'

The tension started to flow out of her. It wasn't ideal, it wasn't the solitude she had hoped for, but with people around them at a party she would be safe, because there would be no opportunity for Santino to ask her the type of penetrating questions she was sure he was leading up to.

'You have two possibilities,' he informed her, pulling out his mobile. 'I can take you back to the hotel and you can travel with the cast and crew, or you can come to the restaurant with me…'

His casual tone suggested he didn't care one way or the other what she did.

Kate hid her disappointment. Santino was giving her the option to back out. She should be grateful and take him up on it. What would it look like to the crew and cast if she arrived with him? She should bring this dangerous encounter to an end right now. If she didn't she would be cooped up with Santino in the tiny cabin of a sports car, finding him infinitely more attractive than she had on the first day they met. The one thing she couldn't do was take the risk of falling for Santino all over again. She couldn't take the risk of losing her heart to a man she knew nothing about, a man whose life was a total mystery to her apart from the obvious power and wealth he wielded. What she should do was go back to the hotel and travel to the party on the coach like everyone else. 'I should be there…'

'Where? Where should you be, Kate?' Santino pressed.

There was something in his eyes Kate recognised, and it made her heart beat faster. 'I should be with you,' she murmured. 'As Caddy's representative.' The words blundered out as reality streamed back into her thinking. 'And as your temporary assistant it would be appropriate for us to greet Diane Fox together,' she said, quickly composing herself.

'My thoughts exactly.' He was breaking down the barriers one by one. He would get to the truth about Kate's personal life however long it took. He had come round to thinking that there must be some pain in her past that made it hard for her to open up. No one understood that sort of thing better than he did, but that didn't mean he had any intention of softening towards her.

The moment they settled down in the car sexual tension started snapping between them. He could understand that people might change over five years, but it was harder to understand what game Kate was playing.

'That's better,' he said lightly when she smiled. He judged any reaction better than none.

'Better?'

'Better than seeing you looking so anxious…' He turned up the charm with an indulgent smile. 'You'll have me thinking you're hiding something.'

The expression that came into her eyes now warned him to back off, but that wasn't in his nature. 'You should relax and have fun while you can. It wouldn't hurt you.'

'What kind of fun?'

He eased his shoulders in a shrug. 'Innocent fun… Something tells me you don't have enough of it.' While he was speaking he punched in some numbers on his phone. 'I'm going to call the coach company before we leave here to tell the driver to take everyone straight to the restaurant. We'll all arrive around the same time if they leave now…'

Speaking rapidly in Italian, Santino kept the phone wedged between his ear and shoulder as he secured his seat belt. When he cut the line he placed the phone in its nest, released the handbrake and pulled away.

It was too late to change her mind now, Kate reflected.

The restaurant was an old restored barn with a high, pitched ceiling lined with ancient oak beams. Sound bounced off the vast tiled floor and the floor was packed with tables, every one of which was taken. There was an open kitchen at one end and Santino had been right about the noise. The chefs were yelling at each other and the waiters were yelling at the chefs and everyone else had to yell to be heard above the yelling. Because the studio party was a last minute affair the room hadn't been closed to the general public, though the film crew had commandeered one of the long, refectory-style tables and lined it with ice buckets and jugs of iced water and wine…

'Kate, you're here!' Caddy raced to the door to greet them with a hug for Kate and a big grin for her producer. 'We've only just arrived. You must have driven like the wind, Santino. Isn't this fantastic?'

For a moment Kate couldn't answer. She was shell-shocked by the chaos and it seemed as if teams of children were weaving between the tables, which made her miss Francesca more than ever.

'Nectar,' Santino murmured in her ear. 'And I really don't blame them.'

Kate looked at him in bewilderment, and then realised Santino thought her attention had been drawn to a group of extras exchanging bottles of the studio's Dom Perignon champagne for the local wine.

'I'll make sure you taste some before we leave.'

'Thank you.' She had to relax, but for some reason she couldn't.

'I thought you'd like it here,' Santino went on, unaware of Kate's growing tension. 'It's a perfect fit with your love of the local culture.'

'Yes,' Kate murmured distractedly, glancing around, looking for something, she hardly knew what.

She was being silly. Santino was right. It was nice here. And how could she not like it when his hand was planted in the small of her back as he began to steer her across the room? If only his hand didn't fit quite so well... If only it weren't such a struggle to keep her thoughts confined to business...

She wasn't here to flirt with Santino, she was here to meet Diane Fox and look after Caddy, Kate reminded herself firmly. But where was Diane Fox, and where had Caddy got to?

They had almost reached the table the film company had commandeered when Caddy appeared out of nowhere at her elbow. At the same moment Kate froze.

'Don't you like your surprise, Kate?'

Kate heard Caddy's question, but was unable to answer. She could only stare transfixed down the room to where a little girl, having spotted her mother, was racing to greet her…

It took him a moment to put his brain into gear when an older woman came to stand between him and Kate. She was vaguely bohemian in appearance and her soft grey eyes were kind and full of concern. She had to be Kate's legendary Aunt Meredith, he realised.

'Oh, Kate,' she exclaimed softly, putting a hand on Kate's arm, 'I'm so sorry. I didn't mean to shock you. I should have rung to warn you we were coming, but it was so last minute there wasn't chance. It was Caddy's idea. She said you were feeling down. I hope I've done the right thing?'

He was still staring at the woman when the bottom fell out of his world. A beautiful dark-haired child of about four years old threw herself at Kate, and as she swept her into her arms and met his gaze above the black glossy curls he knew.

Kate paled as she clutched the child closer to her chest, and it ripped out his heart to see the terror in her eyes, but that was nothing compared to the feelings inside him.

Instantly aware, instantly curious, the child lifted her head to study him. Lodging her thumb in her mouth, she nestled closer to her mother while Caddy and Meredith melted away. He was vaguely aware of the demands on him pulling him this way and that, but as Kate remained frozen in a tableau he couldn't tear his gaze from he knew that nothing else mattered but this.

Kate planted a fervent kiss on her daughter's black curls. *His daughter!* There wasn't a shred of doubt in his mind. The child was his, every inch of her a Rossi…the high colour, the cheek-bones, the jet-black hair, the curls, the luminous brown eyes that stared straight into his soul. She was his child, his daughter, his baby, the first and only member of his family. He went cold to think of all the years that had been stolen from him…from both of them. *And he didn't even know her name.*

'Mummy…' She tugged at Kate's sleeve. 'Who is this man? I like him.'

His heart shattered and fell in pieces at his daughter's feet. Anger, anger such as he had never known, was rising deep inside him. He should have known that this was the reward you got for even thinking about trusting a woman.

'Say hello to your daddy, Francesca.'

Francesca…Francesca…Francesca…

'Hello,' his daughter said solemnly.

Kate was desperate for him to look at her, for him to offer her some reassurance, but he only had eyes for the child…the child reaching out to him.

To him.

CHAPTER NINE

KATE'S heart was pounding so hard she could barely breathe, but she had to make everything seem completely normal for Francesca's sake. 'Shall we sit down?'

This was the worst of all possible outcomes, and, however well he handled it, it had to have been a terrible shock for Santino. Without preamble, or explanation, he discovered they had a daughter together. But she could hardly blame Caddy or Meredith for doing what they believed was in her best interest.

Kate made for a free table, conscious that Francesca was leaning over her shoulder wanting Santino to carry her, but Kate wasn't ready for that yet.

'Is that why you came to Rome, Mummy...to find Daddy?' Francesca asked Kate as they sat down.

'Not exactly...' 'Kate couldn't lie. She hadn't lied to Francesca yet, and she had no intention of making this the start of some new regime. 'Remember what I told you?' Kate swung Francesca onto her knees so she could look into her eyes. 'I came to Rome to see Aunty Caddy—'

'So did Aunty Caddy find Daddy for me?' Francesca turned and levelled a long, considering stare on Santino.

'No, I found you,' Santino said, smiling as he came to sit down beside Kate.

Kate felt a chill run through her. Santino wouldn't meet her gaze. She was dead to him. His attention was focused on his daughter to the exclusion of everything else and Francesca was equally intent on him. For the first time in Francesca's life Kate felt shut out, which frightened her and made her think it was a terrible foretaste of the future.

Francesca chattered on and when she paused for breath Santino suggested they call Meredith over. It was the moment Kate knew had to come, but had been dreading.

'I'd like to speak privately with your mummy,' he told Francesca, 'and then afterwards you and I will have chance to get to know each other a little better.'

Francesca smilingly agreed, but Kate couldn't lose the feeling that Santino's words contained a threat aimed in her direction. She was loath to leave the table to go and look for Meredith, but Santino had left her with little option. The moment she stood up to leave the table Francesca climbed up on Santino's knee.

Hovering close to the table, Kate felt numb as she watched the two of them together. Father and daughter...dark hair, dark eyes, even the same smile, it was uncanny. Everything had happened so quickly, too quickly, before she'd had chance to consider whether Santino might make a suitable father for Francesca. And now it was too late. Francesca was instantly besotted with her father, and Santino was equally enchanted by his beautiful daughter. There was no going back now. But in fairness she couldn't fault Santino's behaviour. Even though he had to be at breaking point no one would ever have guessed it.

'Are you going to find Meredith?' he prompted, and as he turned to look at her Kate jerked back to full attention.

'Yes, of course.' His voice had been carefully pitched not

to alarm Francesca, but the expression in Santino's eyes, which Francesca could not see, chilled Kate to the bone. 'I'll go and look for her now…' But the truth was, she didn't want to leave them alone for a moment. She felt instantly threatened by the closeness that had sprung up between them within moments of them meeting.

'Francesca will be quite safe with me.'

Santino's words held a threat, but Kate knew she had to remain calm. She mustn't let Santino see how intimidated he made her feel. 'I'll only be a moment.' She directed the words at Francesca. 'Stay there and Mummy will be back before you know it.'

It was the best she could do without causing an unpleasant scene, and what hurt most of all was that Francesca hardly noticed her leaving. She had already turned away to Santino and was chatting to him as if all the years that divided them had simply melted away.

Would Santino ever allow Francesca to leave his side again? Kate wondered fearfully as she rushed about the room searching for Cordelia and Meredith. Every second was a second too long for her to be parted from her precious daughter. Kate felt as if her life depended on finding her cousin and her aunt and getting back to Francesca, which it did, because Francesca was her life and always would be.

She was so adept at finding solutions to other people's problems, but here in the middle of a crisis in her own life she was floundering, Kate realised with agonised frustration. The future was a blank canvas upon which only Santino could draw, while she couldn't see her way past this nightmare. The only certainty was that everything would change now that Santino was part of her life again. The enmity springing off him had been both a warning and a foretaste of the future.

She found Caddy chattering away in the centre of an admiring crowd, blissfully unaware of the crisis she had created. Kate didn't want to disturb her when she could see Caddy was talking to an older woman Kate realised must be the director Diane Fox. But thankfully Meredith, having spotted her, quickly extricated herself from the group.

'Kate?'

'Meredith, I'm so sorry… I haven't even said hello to you.' She'd hardly acknowledged her at all, Kate realised, giving her favourite aunt a distracted hug. 'Do you think you could look after Francesca for me for a few minutes while I talk to Santino?'

'I'd be pleased to…' Meredith took a closer look at Kate. 'Kate, what's wrong?'

'Nothing,' Kate lied shakily. 'Santino wants to speak to me in private.'

'That's good news, isn't it?' Meredith put a comforting hand on Kate's arm.

Meredith was so naïve; she always thought the best of everyone and Kate couldn't ever be angry or impatient with her. 'Yes, I'm sure it's an excellent sign,' she said with a smile to reassure her aunt.

When Kate and Meredith arrived back at the table they found Francesca asleep in Santino's arms. The sight stunned Kate. She wondered if she had ever felt quite so cold, or so heartsick and threatened.

'The travelling must have exhausted her,' Meredith exclaimed fondly, holding out her arms to take Francesca.

'We have a lot of catching up to do, *piccola*,' Santino murmured as he handed a sleeping Francesca over with the greatest care to Meredith.

Catching up to do… Santino's words echoed eerily in Kate's head, and made her fear for the future. He was right—

Santino did have a lot of catching up to do and so did Francesca. And how could she deny them time together? She couldn't forget the influence Santino wielded, or the fact that she had no contacts in Rome or in London. She had no one she could call on in a tug of love situation. She would have to pick a lawyer out of a book like pinning the tail on a donkey…taking her chances that she picked a good one like the rest of humanity.

Kate couldn't fail to be moved by the depth of emotion on Santino's face as he watched Meredith carry Francesca away, but it was that same reflection of possession and entitlement that filled her with dread. She wasn't frightened of Santino in a physical sense, but as he rose to his feet and towered over her she felt herself shrink inwardly.

He stood looking down at her in silence, and when he spoke his voice was low and full of menace. 'How could this happen, Kate?'

'Please, Santino, not here…' She found it hard to vocalize, her throat had seized up so badly with fright. She wasn't even certain that Santino heard her as she started for the door.

'Kate…'

Sensing Santino behind her, Kate was suddenly consumed by a primeval fear. She started running, her feet drumming on the wooden floor, adding to the noise in the room, and that noise reverberated in her head, driving her feet, stealing her breath until she was almost blind with panic by the time she reached the exit. She had to fight her way through the crowd to get out, but people coming into the restaurant hardly noticed and were still smiling as she jostled them. They had a party to go to, friends to meet, food to eat, wine to drink, while Kate was lost in a nightmare without end.

As she burst through the door she was sobbing and had to

pause for breath before she could set off again and run down the path. Clutching her throat, she gulped in the warm clean air, but Santino caught up with her too quickly before she could compose herself.

'Please, Santino, please…' His grip on her arm was remorseless.

'Let's get one thing straight before we go any further.' He thrust her in front of him and his eyes were molten with rage as he stared down at her. 'Francesca *is* my daughter.'

It was a statement, not a question, Kate realised, and one prompted entirely by male pride. But she had pride too and she was incensed on Francesca's behalf that her parentage should be drawn into question. 'Yes, of course she is!' She answered him back furiously. 'Any fool can see that.'

Santino stiffened, causing Kate to jerk back, but there was only disgust on his face.

'No need to ask who's been the fool,' he said icily.

'All I'm trying to say is there's no mistaking the fact that Francesca is your child. You must know she is.'

'As you have known for four long years. And must have known you were pregnant five years ago—' Santino broke off with a sound of contempt and walked away as if he couldn't bring himself to look at her a moment longer. He didn't stop walking until he reached a place that was shaded by the overhanging branches of an ancient tree. And then he turned and Kate was shaken by the force of his venomous stare.

'*Non posso crederio,* Kate! I can't believe it!' Santino's voice was harsh, his gaze impenetrable. 'I can't believe you would do this to me!'

Kate had never heard a voice made so ugly by emotion, or seen a face so deeply wounded she had no option but to look away. This was Santino in the raw, with all semblance of civilisation stripped away from him. The charm and civility he was renowned for were nowhere to be seen. The consideration for her sex had utterly deserted him. Santino had never seemed more dominant to her than he did at this moment, or more intimidating. She could see now that he posed a terrible threat to the simple life she enjoyed with Francesca, and would remain a threat unless she could find some way to placate him…

He levelled a steely gaze on her face. 'I asked you a question, which as yet you have not seen fit to answer. I can guess your reply…you'll find some excuse.'

'If you'd only let me explain…' She reached out to him. 'Please, Santino, why won't you listen to me?'

'So you can tell me more lies? I'm done with listening to you, Kate. It's your turn to listen to me. And I'm telling you…' his voice dropped to a menacing whisper… 'you… owe…me…the truth.'

'I realise I should have told you before, but—'

'But?' Santino bit out. 'I asked you how could this happen and you prepare to feed me some excuse?' His voice was like a shard of glass, cruel and sharp. 'How long have you been in Rome, Kate? How many times have we sat together? How many opportunities have there been when you could have told me about Francesca? How many chances have you ignored? You could have told me today. You could have told me five years ago. You could have found me then if you had really wanted to.'

'I was eighteen.'

He gave a contemptuous laugh. 'Don't plead your age as an excuse. You were old enough to go to bed with me—and as I remember you didn't take much persuading.' Turning his face to the sky, he exhaled raggedly as if he had hoped to find the answer there.

There were no words to touch Santino's grief and nothing Kate could do to stop the memories flooding into her mind, memories that only reminded her in the cruellest way possible that Francesca was all she had left now. Meredith and Caddy were wonderful, but the bond between a mother and child was like no other... It could fill you with the most tremendous joy, or break you with unimaginable sorrow. But she couldn't think about that now. She had to find a way to reach Santino or risk losing Francesca.

Even as Santino brutalised her with words there was so much she wanted to say to him, so much she wanted to share, so much he should be told. So much that tragically, now, would always be left unsaid. What was the point in heaping more pain and grief on top of the rest? What was the point in confiding in a man who didn't want to hear what she had to say? She had known too much loss to risk more. She had to think about Francesca now and remember how lucky she was, and not stare backwards into the past longing for what was lost.

Kate's anxiety levels rose as Santino started walking away. 'Where are you going?' But she could see where he was going. He was heading back towards the restaurant where Francesca was waiting. Who knew what he might do? Anything was possible. She ran after him and grabbed his arm.

He shook her off angrily. 'Don't try to stop me going to my daughter. Just get away from me.'

She was no longer required, here, or in his organisation, or in his life. But retreat wasn't an option and so she ran after him again. 'Santino... Please, I know how hurt you must be—'

'You have no idea,' he assured her without breaking stride.

'Please, Santino, for Francesca's sake, we must—'

'*We?*' He stopped dead. 'There is no *we*. Surely you don't imagine I would trust you with the smallest decision where my daughter is concerned?'

Kate had started to shake uncontrollably. 'You have to listen to me, Santino. You have no choice.'

'No choice?' He smiled at her in a way that made her quake. 'Is that a fact?'

'I am Francesca's mother—'

'Yes, her *mother?*' Santino declared with scorn. 'And like all mothers you think only of yourself.'

His comment filled Kate's mind with unanswered questions. As he started to walk away she ran and stood in front of him again.

He made an angry gesture as if to brush her aside. 'Like all women, you think you can lie and cheat and get away with it, don't you, Kate?'

He gave her no chance to respond. But as each cruel accusation rained down on her Kate found that, instead of being frightened, she was filled with the unnatural calm of a person who had nothing left to lose. 'Is this what you'll tell our daughter when Francesca grows to be a woman?' Kate's voice was laced with sadness and for the first time she noticed Santino's gaze shift uncomfortably. 'You asked me how this could happen.' Kate took a deep breath. The last thing she wanted was Santino's pity, but for Francesca's sake she had to do this. 'When my parents discovered I was pregnant they threw me out of the house. Aunt Meredith took me in—'

'And still you didn't think to try and find me?' Santino swiftly returned to the attack. 'Even when you were safe with your aunt you didn't think to tell me I had a daughter? No, why should you? You had assumed that I was the worst type of man. You had decided I would turn my back on you. You didn't give me a chance. Why should you tell me anything when your life with Meredith was so comfortable?'

'Don't bring Meredith into this,' Kate warned. Fire flooded back into her veins as she leapt to her aunt's defence. 'Meredith has never done you any harm and she is a most wonderful grandmother for Francesca. I won't have you run her down—'

'You're in no position to make demands on me, but I apologise to Meredith.' Santino's tone left Kate in no doubt that she was excluded from his magnanimous gesture.

How could she have done things any differently? Should she have told Santino about Francesca five years ago when the gossipmongers had still been chewing over the latest woman to accuse him of fathering her child? Should she have exposed Francesca to the repercussions of that in later life when she might be taunted by old newspaper accounts? Should she have thrown herself on the mercy of a man she didn't know? Should she have run the risk that Santino would claim Francesca and turn his back on her, as her own parents had done?

Kate still believed she had done the right thing, because whatever she had done wrong or imperfectly she had maintained stability in Francesca's life and she wouldn't apologise for that. 'I didn't think you'd want to know, and so I made the only decision I could under the circumstances.'

'You made decisions that weren't yours to make. You set yourself up in judgement over me. What gave you that right? Who are you to decide if I should or shouldn't be told that I have a child? I had a right to know about Francesca, and she had a right to know I am her father. You should have tried to find me immediately. You should have appointed a legal representative to raise the matter at a court of law in Rome—'

'A court of law in Rome?' Kate cut across Santino, shuddering inwardly as she imagined the outcome if she had tried to do so. She only had to look into his cold, dark eyes to know she wouldn't have stood a chance. 'Are you suggesting a single mother without money or influence should have tried to take on the Roman establishment? Can't you understand that all I was interested in was keeping my baby safe?'

'And I would have harmed her?' Santino's expression grew blacker than ever. 'You're full of excuses, but all I can see is that you cheated me of my daughter and you cheated Francesca out of her father—'

'That's not true!' Kate was stung to the quick by Santino's accusation that she would do anything to hurt Francesca. 'It wasn't like that! I didn't know you, Santino. I didn't know what type of man you were—'

'You weren't so scrupulous five years ago in my bed!'

They both stiffened and turned reluctantly as Caddy came outside to look for them.

'Diane Fox,' Santino remembered, cursing softly under his breath. 'We have to go back inside. We have to make everything seem normal. We have to be civil to my new director and make our introductions as if nothing had occurred.'

'No, Santino, I can't.'

'You must,' he insisted harshly.

In this he was right, Kate accepted. The last thing Francesca needed was the whole world knowing that Santino Rossi and Kate Mulhoon shared a colourful past. Kate knew it was imperative she put all this to one side and act as if there were nothing between them other than a working relationship. And so when Caddy waved and called out to them she smiled, and when they walked inside together she and Santino greeted everyone with practised charm and total professionalism.

Kate was on automatic pilot for the next few hours, maintaining the smile on her face and pretending interest in everything and everyone. But she couldn't forget Santino's bitter words or the threat behind them, and they continued to override everything else in her mind. She had to remind herself time after time that she had a job to do. Caddy needed someone to take care of the minutiae of her life so she could shine more brightly and Kate had always been happy to do that. Nothing had changed, she told herself firmly. Santino couldn't take Francesca away from her. There wasn't a court in the world that would allow him to do that.

Kate was relieved to find her first impression of the new director was positive. Diane Fox had a firm handshake and a warm smile, but when she turned to reassure herself that Francesca and Meredith were still where she had left them Kate saw Santino standing with them…and Francesca had woken up…and now Santino was leading them to a secluded corner where he could hold a conversation with his daughter in private. The two of them were animated and obviously enjoying each other's company… Meredith was trailing behind…smiling, unaware of the threat. Excusing herself from the group that had gathered around Diane Fox, Kate hurried over to them.

'And then I fell off…' Seeing Kate, Francesca held out her arms automatically, waiting to be lifted into her mother's arms. 'The naughty pony bucked me off, Mummy,' she explained, bringing her face close to Kate's ear.

It was a simple admission and probably a tall story, for surely Meredith would have said something, but it was enough to make Santino look at her as if Francesca's innocent explanation was further proof that Kate was unfit to be a mother. Bringing Francesca into her arms, Kate was overcome by fear that if a custody battle reached court it might not have the outcome she hoped for. Burying her face in Francesca's fragrant, silky hair, she held her daughter close as if she would never let her go.

CHAPTER TEN

SANTINO glanced at his watch. 'We should be going home, Francesca.'

'Oh, will you be taking us back to the hotel?' Meredith chipped in, oblivious to the undercurrents. 'That is kind of you, Santino.'

'My home,' he emphasised.

Meredith looked bewildered, and Kate felt the chill in Santino's gaze as he stared her down.

'Please don't do this,' Kate urged softly, transferring Francesca to Meredith's arms. 'Let's not argue about where we go from here, Santino.' Kate quickly added a small laugh for Francesca's sake, though her words were loaded and all the adults present knew it.

A flash of alarm crossed Meredith's face, but she quickly controlled it and adapted to the situation, lifting Francesca high in the air to distract her. 'Let's go, pigeon. I'll take Francesca to get her coat while you two sort out your business.'

Full marks to Meredith, Kate thought, relieved to see Francesca was still smiling and completely unaware of the tension between her parents.

'Santino, please,' Kate said the moment they were out of

earshot. 'Don't try to take Francesca from me now. Can't you see how happy she is? Do you want to upset her?'

'Of course I don't.' Santino's face turned from cold to gentle in the time it took him to turn his head to watch Francesca walking through the lines of tables hand in hand with Meredith. He even smiled when Francesca turned to wave at him, but where Kate was concerned, she might not have been there.

Something terrible must have happened to him in his youth and she should try to understand so she could find a way to touch his heart. But softening towards a man who planned to take Francesca from her was a terrible risk.

Meredith and Francesca had just disappeared into the cloakroom and Santino watched every step they took intently. This was not the man she had been learning to like and trust Kate realised, the man she had harboured dreams of falling in love with. This was another man, another Santino. This was the ruthless businessman, the warrior who must win every battle at whatever cost. How could she fight a man like that?

'Francesca will be coming home with me.'

'What do you mean?' Kate's heart stopped. She knew what he meant. Santino was talking about his home. And how could she stop him? She couldn't fight him. She couldn't risk Francesca being subjected to an ugly scene between her parents. The only thing she could do was appeal to Santino's better nature and hope he had one. 'She's a little girl, Santino. Don't make her part of this fight between us…'

His mouth flattened with determination. 'You don't seem to understand. I've got almost five years to make up for. I want to see my daughter when she wakes in the morning.'

Even now with all the enmity rising between them there was something in his eyes, and in his voice, that cut Kate to the bone, but then his voice hardened to something that inspired fear rather than sympathy.

'I'm surprised that you of all people can't understand what I'm trying to say. And you a *mother*.'

He made the word mother sound so ugly Kate knew it threatened everything she held dear.

'I'm going to be with my daughter. I'm going to see her every moment of the day. I'm going to laugh with her and have fun with her. I'm going to have a life with her.' Santino's eyes were flint hard when they turned on her. 'Or would you deny me that as well?'

She couldn't help herself and reached out, but he backed away as if he couldn't bear her to touch him. 'Santino, please… If you take Francesca away from me now it won't help your cause if she wakes up tomorrow in an unfamiliar place surrounded by strangers—'

'I'm her father, not a stranger.'

'And Francesca's a little girl who is half asleep after a tiring journey. Are you prepared to take the risk that she'll remember you when she wakes up tomorrow? Please let her stay with me tonight, and I promise I'll bring her to you—'

'Like you did before? Am I supposed to trust you now?'

The fight went out of Kate as the past came back to haunt her. 'Don't do this to me, Santino. Not again…please…I'm begging you… Don't take my baby… She's everything to me—'

'Your tears are wasted on me.'

'I promise you—'

'You promise me?'

'Please don't take my baby, Santino.' Kate grabbed his arm as he moved away. 'She's all I have—'

'Then you have more than I do,' he assured her coldly. 'Now please take your hands off my sleeve.'

Santino's arm felt rigid beneath her touch as Kate pulled her hands away. 'I'm sorry.'

'You will be,' Santino promised her.

She scrambled after him, terrified to think that Santino didn't trust her and never would again. 'I can't blame you—'

'Spare me your pity!' He brushed her aside and walked on.

'I'm the one asking for your pity…' Remembering what was at stake, Kate ran after him. 'For our daughter's sake, Santino, I'm pleading with you—'

'You're making an embarrassing show of yourself.' Santino halted abruptly, turning to confront her. 'Shake yourself out of it before anyone notices.' His mouth curled with disdain as he stared down at her. 'And then stay away from me.'

But she couldn't do that. She wouldn't do that. Kate stood her ground. A couple of people had glanced their way, then looked away again. This was the film world where high drama was an everyday occurrence and everyone was having too good a time at the party to pay much attention to the isolated drama being played out on the fringes. 'You're not taking her from me… You can't—'

'I shall be applying for full custody of Francesca…' Santino's voice held a note she had never heard before. 'If you want to see more of your daughter you have two choices. You either see her in the school holidays, or you move to Italy where access will be easier for you. But don't think for one moment that this is a battle I intend to lose. No court in the world is going to refuse me when I point out how irresponsible Francesca's mother has been…how reckless she was when we first met, and how reckless she is now…staying away, leaving our child in the care of an elderly aunt…' He held up his hand when Kate's ashen lips began to move. 'Yes, Kate, everything they say about me is true. I stop at nothing to get what I want. And where my daughter's concerned you can expect me to pull out all the stops.'

'You're a monster,' Kate managed faintly.

'A monster?' Santino appeared to find her accusation amusing. 'Come now, Kate… Any judge would recognise me as a father who loves his daughter and wants to protect her from harm…a loving father who wants to make up for all the lost years denied to me by her mother.'

As she saw the truth in his words he could sense her defeat. He would make one concession, and only because Francesca might be alarmed by the sudden loss of her mother. He would not subject his daughter to the pain he had known as a child, therefore any parting would have to be gradual. Decision made, he found Kate's continued dejection irritating. 'Try to remember you still work for me. I need you to make a phone call…' He exhaled with impatience when she didn't respond. 'For goodness' sake, pull yourself together. While I spend a few moments with Diane Fox I need you to telephone the hotel—'

'The hotel?'

She looked up at that and he saw the pain in her eyes. She was still reeling from the news that he intended to take Francesca away from her, but this was no time for misplaced sympathy. She'd had five years on the run before he'd caught up with her and now she could pay the penalty. 'You will ask if they have another suite available. Call them,' he said brusquely. 'Tell them who it's for, and that we need two bedrooms.'

'We? I thought there was no we,' she managed faintly.

Barely any sound came out of her mouth, but she was still fighting him. Part of him admired that, but the more dominant part of him rolled on seamlessly with his plan. 'I require a twin-bedded room for you and Francesca, and another room for me.'

Hope flared in her eyes as he mentioned the room she

would share with Francesca and died again the moment she realised that he would be standing guard.

'This is not for your benefit,' he confirmed, content to see despair replace the brief flash of hope in her eyes, 'but for Francesca's sake. I intend that any parting from you will be gradual.'

'You're very kind.'

Her dumb insolence infuriated him. She was letting him know that as far as she was concerned the torture he intended to inflict upon her would only be prolonged.

'I doubt the Russie is full,' she said, slowly recovering. 'I'll ring them now and ask if another suite could be made available.'

'You only have to mention my name,' he reminded her, driving the last nail in the coffin home.

Of course there was a suite available. For Signor Rossi, Kate was informed, anything was possible. She winced as the well-meaning reservations clerk said this, while Santino's cold dark eyes bored into her. The expression on Santino's face went so far beyond dislike what she really wanted to do was run as far and fast as she could from him, but she would never leave Francesca. As she cut the line Kate made one last plea. 'You're Francesca's father Santino. There's a bond between you that no one can break, not even me. I'm no threat to you. Can't you see that?'

'Did you tell the hotel to hold the suite?' Santino's voice was expressionless.

'Of course I did.'

'Then you'd better speak to Cordelia and Meredith to let them know what's happening.' Turning on his heel he walked away.

* * *

The suite was grand and luxurious. Nothing but the best for Signor Rossi, the hotel manager had been at pains to advise Kate. And as it happened the presidential suite was unoccupied that evening…

Every turn she took offered up more proof of the power Santino wielded and what she was up against, Kate thought as she switched off the bedside light. She settled on her side to listen to Francesca breathing, deeply conscious that Santino was pacing the floor in the other bedroom. Francesca was so innocent and so defenceless and had no idea what was going on. She only knew that it was fun sleeping in a twin bed beside her mother with her father in the next room. She had to keep it that way, Kate determined. Right now Francesca had everything in the world to look forward to and nothing was going to change that—not even Santino Rossi.

Pulling herself up on one elbow to stare at her daughter, Kate made a silent pledge that Francesca's happiness would remain her primary concern. There had been no men passing in and out of her life, because all she cared about was Francesca and she would defend her daughter to the last breath in her body. She could only hope that one day Santino might learn to have a different view of the bond that existed between a mother and her child.

As she settled down again for what she knew would be a restless night's sleep Kate pulled the duvet over her head to shut out the sound of Santino in the room next door. She knew he was pacing in an attempt to eat up the hours before dawn when he could wake up his legal team and turn his threats towards her into reality.

As she had expected Kate slept fitfully. There were so many possibilities to consider, so many potential pitfalls to prepare for. She woke at first light when it seemed she had only just fallen asleep to find Francesca already awake and playing with her teddy.

'Is teddy hungry?' Kate asked sleepily, knowing it was essential she make things seem as normal as possible for Francesca.

'Yes, and he's complaining.' Francesca held the scruffy toy to her ear.

'I'm sure we can find him something.' Kate was halfway out of bed when the knock came on the door.

'Who is it, Mummy? Gran Meredith, or Aunty Caddy?'

Kate's heart thundered as she held a finger to her lips. Just as she had feared and had tried in the gentlest way to explain before Santino had turned nasty, in an unfamiliar setting a child always clung to the familiar. 'Don't you remember who came to see you yesterday?' Kate whispered, fearful that Santino would overhear her.

'Who?' Francesca demanded, launching herself from the bed.

At that moment Kate might have felt triumphant or smug, but she felt neither. Even after the terrible things Santino had said to her she still loved him and as a parent her heart went out to him. Knowing Santino was standing behind the door full of hope waiting to see a daughter who after such a brief acquaintance had already forgotten him filled her with sadness for everything they'd lost, and it was for Francesca's sake that Kate called out brightly, 'Just a minute. We'll be right with you.'

This was the defining moment, Kate realised, and she had to handle it well, not just for Francesca's sake, but for Santino's too. She couldn't bring herself to hurt him any more than she already had. However hard the face he turned towards her was, there wasn't a convenient switch to turn off the love she felt for him.

She commenced the charade by drawing Francesca close. 'Well? Who do you think is waiting to see you behind that door?'

Francesca wiped an arm across her face. And then, remembering, she gave a little leap in Kate's arms. 'My daddy!'

'That's right, my darling…' It was time to let Francesca go. She would come back if she wanted to. Kate had to learn to share her with Santino. But as she watched Francesca racing for the door Kate felt as if her heart had been ripped out of her chest and laid on the ground for Santino to trample on.

Kate could only commend Santino's behaviour as they sat together like a proper family eating breakfast in their private dining room. No one but the most acute observer would suspect a problem. Kate knew that, like her, Santino hadn't slept well, but he was charming to the waiters and vastly entertaining to his daughter, if Francesca's delighted chuckles were anything to go by.

'And I'm going to show you how well I ride, Daddy.'

'What a good idea…' Santino grew thoughtful. 'I have a place in the country not far from Rome—'

'A cottage like Gran Meredith's!' Francesca clapped her hands with excitement. 'I love cottages. When can we go, Mummy? Can we go today? Do you have horses?' she added, turning to Santino without pausing for breath.

'Yes, I do, as it happens,' he confirmed, glancing at Kate.

But his eyes when he looked at her were cold, and his expression was one of dislike. If they went to Santino's home Kate knew she would only be there under sufferance. But at least it would give her a little more time to work out how she was going to handle the changes that were sure to come. 'Why don't I speak to Caddy on the phone and see if she can spare me? And then I'll ask Meredith if she would be kind enough to accompany us…' Kate hoped she had made it clear that wherever Francesca went, until she was prevented by force, or by law, she went too.

'Very well,' Santino agreed after a nerve-racking, hate-filled silence. 'I'll make my plans accordingly…'

Kate jolted back to attention. They had turned in at some rather grand gates and a long, straight road stretched in front of them. There were lush green fields on either side and the well-maintained road was lined with stately cedar trees. Santino had made one quick phone call from their suite and a Range Rover had been delivered to the door. Now Meredith was sitting in the back with Francesca, while Kate was sitting stiffly in the front next to Santino wrapped in thoughts of visitation rights and lawyers. There were so many avenues to explore when it came to Francesca's future, and with Santino ranged against her Kate knew she risked all of them turning into dead ends unless she secured the best possible legal advice.

Santino hadn't addressed a single word to her throughout the journey, though he maintained an easy conversation with Meredith and Francesca. Kate kept telling herself that it was crucial not to feel defeated at this stage, but that was easier said than done when she felt sick inside with apprehension.

She had received one piece of good news. Caddy had rung the room before they left to say that Diane Fox had decided all the actors must go off site to a retreat where she could explain her vision to them. Kate had almost cheered, knowing it left her free.

'When we turn this last corner you will see my home in the country.'

Kate's attention returned to Santino, who was talking to Francesca and Meredith. His face was angled towards them, but when his gaze grazed Kate's face the smile died.

Meredith appeared oblivious to the tension between them and launched in with a stream of questions connected to the house they were about to visit. Santino took it in his stride, explaining that the vast country estate had been in someone else's family for centuries, but that now it was his. For the dynasty he intended to create, he said, laughing softly as he turned to Meredith. Meredith laughed with him, and, infected by their mood, Francesca joined in. Only Kate remained silent.

The wedge between them was greater than ever. How could she ever compete with this? She had always known Santino was a wealthy man, but privilege on this scale was unimaginable until you experienced it. And Francesca saw the world through a child's eyes. How could she fail to be impressed by her father's circumstances?

Fear tore through Kate as she thought about the future. Even though Meredith was chattering away as if there were nothing to worry about, Kate couldn't lose the feeling of dread growing inside her. And Meredith was no measure to go by—she was always enthused by new ideas and open to possibilities… *Such as bringing Francesca to Rome on the lightest pretext?*

Nothing would surprise Kate where her unconventional aunt was concerned, but this was the first time Meredith's judgement had proved to be so severely flawed.

'Well, what do you think?' Santino said as they turned a final corner.

Meredith and Francesca gasped as the mellow walls of

Santino's gracious country home came into view. He had been happy to go along with Francesca's idea that he lived in a cosy country cottage not dissimilar to Meredith's. But if this was a cottage…Kate shook her head in incredulity. A cottage like le Petit Trianon perhaps, made famous by the ill-fated Queen of France, Marie Antionette…

'It's a big cottage, Daddy,' Francesca observed solemnly. 'Do the horses live inside with you?'

There was certainly room for them, Kate reckoned. She wanted to crane her neck and take everything in, but she didn't want to give Santino the opportunity to accuse her of valuing his assets, and so she held back.

'No,' Santino said in answer to Francesca, 'the horses live in the stable yard at the rear of the *palazzo*. Would you like me to drive you straight there so you can see them?'

Francesca's excitement was all the answer he needed, and even Meredith joined in the fun. Only Kate was excluded from the enthusiastic chorus. She felt invisible, or as if she was the only person present who wasn't a member of the Santino Rossi fan club. But then she hadn't been invited to join, Kate reminded herself, trying to relax.

When he stopped the car Santino sprang out to open the rear door where Francesca was sitting. That was Kate's job. She always helped Francesca to release the restraints on her car seat and jump down to the ground, making sure she didn't tumble…

'Don't they look lovely together?'

Sensing her tension, Meredith had put a comforting hand on Kate's arm as they stood together at the side of the vehicle. Kate knew Meredith's hand on her arm was meant as a stay too. And she knew she shouldn't begrudge Santino his time with Francesca. But she did, because every moment he spent with her cemented the bond between them and made it that much easier for him to cut Francesca's mother out of her life. It was a struggle for her to hold back and watch them walking away from her hand in hand.

Kate grew more fearful as she listened to Francesca's excited exclamations as Santino led his daughter down the line of stables. Noble heads peered curiously over each half open door and she had to keep telling herself not to be so mean-minded and to be glad for Francesca. But what she really wanted was to be a million miles away from the immaculately kept yard, to take Francesca somewhere, anywhere, that Santino couldn't find them.

When the tour had been completed Santino brought Francesca back to Kate's side. 'Well, what do you think?' he said to his little daughter.

Francesca's brow wrinkled as she thought about it. 'They're all very big. Too big for me.'

'True…' Cupping his chin, Santino pretended to think about it. 'It's a shame I don't have a pony for you to ride, or we could have gone riding together.'

'Really?' As Francesca's eyes widened Santino met Kate's gaze over their daughter's head.

If this was intended as a warning to her it had succeeded, Kate thought, but she held his gaze determinedly. She didn't need this power play to understand that Santino could offer Francesca infinitely more in the way of material possessions than she ever could. And Francesca was too young to understand the politics of love. All Francesca knew was that everything she had ever dreamed of was within her reach now she had discovered she had a father like Santino.

'I have arranged for us to go rowing on the lake after lunch,' Santino confided in Francesca. 'Do you think you would enjoy that?'

'A lake? Here?' Francesca gazed about, almost beside herself with excitement now.

'But first you and Gran Meredith can play with the new puppies while Mummy and I have a chat—'

'Puppies!'

Francesca's joy was complete. But Kate noticed concern had crept into Meredith's eyes. There had been a small, but significant change in Santino's voice when he'd referred to Kate, which indicated that things were not going quite as smoothly as her well-meaning aunt had intended. It made Kate wish she could say something to reassure Meredith, but what could she say?

'Puppies,' Kate managed woodenly as she took Francesca's hand. 'Won't that be lovely?'

'Don't squeeze so hard, Mummy. You're hurting me.'

'I'm sorry.' Kate's voice was edged with fear. 'That's the very last thing I meant to do…'

CHAPTER ELEVEN

As THEY walked back towards the house Kate's anxiety rose in direct relation to Santino's growing ease. Like everything else he turned his hand to Santino's adaptation to the role of ideal parent had been wholly successful, and as far as Meredith and Francesca were concerned he was the perfect host. Could anyone be more charming? Or more machiavellian?

Kate could only be grateful when Francesca chose to take her hand as they entered the house. Santino's country mansion was on a scale none of them had experienced before and to Francesca must have seemed both exciting and intimidating. As Santino led the way across the vast marble-tiled hallway Meredith walked close by his side, darting off as usual to exclaim at first this picture and then that ornament... There were so many beautiful things around Kate was dazzled, but she was also intimidated by the sheer scale of Santino's wealth. A man with resources such as these could have the world and everyone in it in his pocket.

'I can't claim credit for anything,' Santino was telling Meredith.

No, he had bought it off the shelf in the same way he thought he could buy a family, Kate thought bitterly. She had moved past fear now to feelings that didn't make her proud, and as Francesca paused to stroke the mane of one of the life-sized stone lions that stood guard at the foot of the stairs her lips formed an angry line as Santino asked Francesca if she would like to give the lions names.

'After all, they're your lions now,' he said, glancing at Kate to rub her nose in it.

Resentment burned inside her as she stared back at him. No doubt Santino had an endless supply of such tempting lures to dangle in front of their daughter, and Francesca's eyes were glowing in awe as she looked up at her father. It was becoming harder every moment for Kate to hide her feelings, and impossible not to feel threatened when she did… *She did*.

After the episode with the lions Francesca held onto Santino's hand as he continued the tour of his house. Determined not to be sidelined, Kate walked with them. Anyone looking at them would imagine they were a happy and uncomplicated family group. And as if to confirm this, the servants were all nodding and smiling as if the whole place had sprung to life now Signor Rossi had returned with his ready-made family.

What had Santino told them? Kate wondered. Had he told them anything, or were his staff simply making assumptions and forming a distorted picture of the truth? And was it only she who could feel the storm clouds brewing?

Santino was so gracious to everyone, but he hadn't glanced her way once. He was adept at showing one face to the world and another to her. But however much he hated her for what she had done they were bound together for ever by Francesca. And on top of that there was the unfathomable link that bound them together whether either of them liked it or not. It had existed since the first moment they had laid eyes on each other and she could feel it at work now… It allowed them to read each other's thoughts and second-guess each other's intentions. And right now that was no comfort to her.

Their last stop was a huge glasshouse, which ran the whole length of one wing of the building. There were so many exotic plants Kate was ready to believe that a jungle had been tamed solely for Santino's amusement. There was a raised water feature in one corner of the structure, and a waterfall that tumbled over giant-sized rocks. The puppies he had mentioned were roaming free on the tiled floors. Double glass doors led straight out onto the lawn, and it was here that Santino split their little group, suggesting Francesca and Meredith take the puppies outside on the grass to play while he talked to Kate.

'Kate?' he said, turning to her, indicating another doorway leading into the house.

The way Santino spoke her name was both careful and clever. Francesca was already on her hands and knees with the puppies, but like every child her ears were keenly tuned to those around her. Knowing that Santino had taken care to shield Francesca from the coldness he felt towards her mother was a reminder to Kate that she must also maintain the same charade.

A shiver ran down Kate's spine as Santino led her back inside. She wasn't interested in looking around as Meredith had done. She knew she was unlikely to be invited to the *palazzo* again. She felt out of place with the weight of privilege all around her, and could almost imagine the echo of command bouncing off the ornate plasterwork…perhaps when other errant women had fallen foul of the wealthy family who had lived here.

It was her turn now to fight for her child in a place where she was already at a disadvantage, a place where she was overwhelmed and distracted by the significance of Francesca's heritage.

'In here…' Santino's voice remained cold, though as always he stood aside politely to allow her to precede him into a room leading off the hall.

It was impossible to remain insensible to the beauty of the room. The walls had silk hangings in the softest duck egg blue, and there was a delicately patterned Aubusson rug, in creams and pinks and gold, that took up most of the floor space. That alone must have been worth a fortune, Kate concluded. The panoramic windows overlooked the lake, and she could hear geese in the distance, calling to each other…

'They're on the island,' Santino said, giving the invisible bond between them a little shake. 'They won't come anywhere near Francesca…'

Automatically she reassured him. 'Francesca knows to take care of herself around geese. Meredith keeps geese at the farmhouse. They make better guards than dogs…' Kate's voice tailed away. The brooding atmosphere in the room reminded her that this was neither the time nor the place to hold a normal conversation.

Santino went to stand by the window as far away from her as possible and they stood in silence for a while. When Santino finally turned to face her Kate was shocked to see his lips were ashen.

'Five years, Kate…' Dark eyes pierced her soul. 'Five years of Francesca's life. That's what you have stolen from me.'

She could never make it up to him. Never. 'Stolen from both of you,' Kate said, holding Santino's gaze. She wasn't going to plead innocence when that clearly wasn't the case. She was guilty. She had denied Francesca and Santino the most basic right of all—to know of each other's existence.

Turning away, Santino passed a hand across his eyes as if he wanted to blot her out. Kate could see the effort it took for him to refocus and control his anger when he turned back to her.

'I can't believe I trusted you. I can't believe I thanked fate for bringing you back to me. What a fool I was. You had no intention of telling me I had a daughter. The only reason you came to Rome was for Cordelia—'

'That was part of it—'

'That was all of it. Don't waste your lies on me. Without fate…and, yes, without Meredith, I wouldn't even have known Francesca existed. You cheated me out of my child and now you must pay.'

'I was going to tell you.'

'When, Kate?' Santino's voice was like tempered steel, sharp and precise. 'When exactly were you going to tell me?'

'When I got to know you a little better… When I knew what kind of man you were. When I knew what kind of father you would make for Francesca.'

'So you're my judge and jury now?'

'You've seen her. You've seen how innocent she is, how defenceless… Surely you're not suggesting I should have handed Francesca over to a man I didn't know?'

'Do you dare set yourself up in judgement over me? Are you trying to tell me I was undergoing some sort of test?' he demanded incredulously. 'A test I have not yet passed?' Ebony brows drew tight over his aquiline nose. 'How dare you question my ability to be a good father? You don't know anything about me—'

'That's right, I don't,' Kate cut in, 'and I had to be certain—'

'Of me?'

'I am Francesca's mother. It's my duty to protect her.'

'Yes, you are her mother,' Santino snarled as if that were one of life's greatest misfortunes.

'Are you saying I should have come to you cap in hand when I was eighteen? Should I have begged you then to acknowledge Francesca? What would you have said to me, Santino? What accusation would you have levelled at me then? I remember a court case and another woman—'

'Another liar,' he cut across her.

'Don't you dare compare me to that woman. I'm not a liar, and I never have been.'

'But you withheld the truth from me.'

More than he knew. And as silence echoed all around them Kate accepted that she couldn't deny Santino's assertion. She could only raise her head and look into his eyes as she remembered that one night of passion, one misplaced teenage dream had given her one of life's greatest gifts with one hand and taken away most cruelly with the other. But out of that traumatic event had come Kate's beautiful daughter Francesca, and even if that earned her Santino's everlasting scorn, she wouldn't change a thing.

It was Francesca's laughter that distracted them, and in spite of all the anger in the room Kate found herself smiling as she looked out of the window. Francesca was skipping across the lawn with the puppies in hot pursuit with Meredith hurrying after her predictably carrying the runt of the litter in her arms…

'She's a good woman…'

Santino's voice startled Kate out of her contemplation. Once again he had read her like a book. But what point was there in that now? It was a gift that was wasted on both of them.

'You're lucky—'

She turned to stare at Santino in surprise. 'Lucky?'

'To have an aunt like Meredith… To have a family.'

'You have a family now,' she reminded him.

'And to ensure that I keep one I've asked my lawyer to come over.' In the space of a heartbeat Santino's manner had changed towards her. It was as if he couldn't wait to stamp out the split second of harmony between them.

'I'm going to speak to him while you're having lunch with Meredith and Francesca. And then it will be your turn, Kate.'

Kate's pulse began to race…from fear of what lay ahead and from the look in Santino's eyes. 'My turn?'

'He should speak to you and tell you what to expect. I'll take Francesca out on the lake while you have your meeting.'

Santino was speaking to her as if it were all cut and dried, Kate realised, clutching her throat. 'But nothing's decided yet?' She couldn't prevent her voice rising in a question.

'This is just a preliminary talk.'

But somehow Kate wasn't reassured and when Santino turned his back on her she realised that what he was really saying was that this was the end of direct communication between them. This was the end, or the beginning of the end, at least. In spite of everything grief rose inside her. She couldn't bear it. She couldn't bear the pain. For a moment as she held herself in check Kate wondered if it would ever be possible to lose the love she had for Santino.

'When you return to England,' he continued without turning to look at her, 'I want you to have the best legal advice there is. And of course I'll pay all your expenses.'

'That's a very generous offer Santino…' Kate's throat felt dry '…but I don't need your money.'

'Pride, Kate?' He turned to face her. 'I thought Francesca was the only thing that mattered to you. I thought she meant everything to you.'

'She does, but I pay my own way. Francesca wants for nothing, and I have never been indebted to anyone in my life.'

'Take my advice and don't allow pride to come before your best interests.'

'And are you to decide what my best interests are?'

'I'm trying to help you.' He shrugged and there was no warmth in his expression. 'But if you can't see it...'

'Well, thank you, Santino, but I have a perfectly good solicitor in England.'

'And I'm advising you to get the best. I have no intention of being labelled a bully.'

'So this is all about your pride?'

'Not at all. For Francesca's sake there can't be any loopholes in the agreement between us. We must both know where we stand.'

'I think I know where I stand.' And she would not allow Santino to direct her life or Francesca's life, simply because he wielded so much power.

'You're overreacting,' he observed in a chilly tone. 'You should learn to keep your emotions in check,'

Was that a threat? Even if it was she couldn't stand by and say nothing. 'Maybe you can do that.' Kate stared into Santino's eyes. 'And maybe that's the difference between us, because when it comes to Francesca I can't remain unfeeling. You frighten me when you make comments like that, Santino. I don't want Francesca growing up to be a cold, unfeeling woman with too much money in the bank and less than nothing in her heart.'

As Kate stood facing him with her jaw rigid with determination it was a cruel reminder of how alike they were. But things had gone too far for reconciliation, and he wouldn't risk losing Francesca a second time even if that meant destroying Kate.

'And as for my speaking with your lawyer after lunch,' she went on, 'well, it's unusual, to say the least, and I thank you for the opportunity. I would like to hear what he has to say so that I can be properly prepared. To that end I would like a full set of papers to take back with me to England.'

'I'll make sure it happens.' He turned to go.

The distance that had developed between them frightened Kate more than all the legal firepower Santino could bring into play. She had to draw him back somehow, but she wouldn't stoop to lay bare her darkest secrets and her deepest grief to win him over. There was one more thing she could try...

He stopped at the door realising she was speaking to him, but in so low a voice he wondered for a moment if she was talking to herself. 'I beg your pardon?' He spoke sharply as he turned to face her again.

'Francesca always knew she had a father, Santino. I never lied to her...'

She had him. He had to stay and hear her out. The smallest detail of Francesca's life was precious to him.

'I never told Francesca you were dead, though it would have been a convenient lie.'

'So what did you tell her?' he pressed without sympathy.

'That I lost touch with her father, but that he loved her very much, and that one day he would come back to her.'

'The fairy tale on top of your version of the truth?' His voice rose in indignation, but the honesty blazing from Kate's face threw him back a little.

'I told Francesca a truth she could understand, a truth that made her feel good about herself. It was a version of the truth that didn't make her feel as if you'd left us or turned your back on us as my parents had done to me.'

'Should I thank you?' he said coldly. 'You're damned by

your own actions, Kate. You made no attempt to find me when Francesca was born.'

'All I knew about you was what I read about in the press. I work in the film industry too. I know what goes on. I couldn't take the chance—'

'That I'd be some debauched billionaire?' Santino's gaze hardened.

'I made a decision to protect Francesca from the day I discovered I was pregnant. And that's a commitment for life, Santino, something you would know nothing about.'

'You didn't give me the opportunity to make that choice.'

'A mother has no choice.'

'And what about honesty and trust? Do neither of those play a part in a mother's thinking?' He already knew the answer to that.

So I'm to bear all the consequences?'

'Consequences?' Sweeping ebony brows rose in amusement as he stared at her. 'It's a bit late to be thinking about consequences now. As I remember that night we were two consenting adults who knew exactly what we were doing. If we hadn't I would never have taken you to my bed.'

'You think you know everything, don't you, Santino? I suppose you knew I was a virgin too.'

Mentally he reeled, but what Kate had told him made him even angrier. 'And you thought so much of your precious virginity you couldn't wait to be rid of it—to the extent that you threw it away on a stranger!'

'I certainly threw it away on you!'

'Is that what you'll tell Francesca when she's older?' Santino demanded in a scathing reminder of Kate's earlier accusation. He waited until he had the satisfaction of seeing the blood drain from her face and then informed her coldly, 'I have arranged for lunch to be served on the terrace overlooking the lake. Your presence there will be solely to reassure Francesca.' His voice was as cold as the ice around his heart. He showed Kate no mercy since she deserved none. 'I suggest you pull yourself together before then. You must be calm when Francesca sees you.'

'I'll be calm, Santino,' Kate assured him, grim-faced.

She would never back down. He knew that from the challenge flaring in her eyes. It made him rail against fate for wanting a woman like Kate Mulhoon, and made him rail against fate a second time because he couldn't trust her or any woman on earth to be the mother of his child.

She couldn't weaken now. The next few hours were crucial to Francesca's future.

Kate had accepted that Santino was part of their lives, but she was equally determined he would not have everything his own way. When she met with his lawyer it was vital she made the right choices and said the right things. Under normal circumstances this wouldn't have been a problem—cool, analytical and determined was a fair description of her working manner. But this was a situation where emotion and love met head-on with a deep-seated need to protect her child and that might cloud her mind. She couldn't risk it, she couldn't allow herself to become exhausted or cowed by Santino and his legal team. She had to remain strong and keep her wits about her as she prepared for the battle of her life.

CHAPTER TWELVE

SOUND was cocooned in the panelled library, reducing the precise, sibilant tones of Santino's lawyer to a disembodied stream of information. Kate sat across from him at a highly polished table to one side of the window, and it was taking all her strength of mind not to turn her head to look out to follow Francesca's progress across the lawn, because Francesca was skipping along at Santino's side holding onto his hand as if she had known him all her life.

'Miss Mulhoon...'

Kate refocused, angling her head to show that she was listening. The lawyer spoke perfect English with only the trace of an Italian accent, and she could hardly accuse him of being unreasonable. He was being as gentle with her as if he had been her own advisor offering counsel following a bereavement, which in some ways this was. A part of her life had been lost for ever.

'As you have requested, Miss Mulhoon, I have prepared a full set of papers for you. You must show them to your advisors on your return to England.'

Kate felt a quiver of apprehension and hesitated before accepting the envelope. In a moment of blind panic she had lied to Santino about knowing a good solicitor. She had never had occasion to use a lawyer before except at work, and they were contract lawyers, specialising in media work.

It was hard to believe things had come to this.

'Thank you,' she said with a flat smile, taking the papers she realised could only have been prepared so quickly if Santino had rung his lawyer the previous night.

That was so typical of Santino. He made a decision and acted immediately. He left nothing to chance—no loose ends, no second thoughts. It chilled Kate to think that a plan had been in place before Santino had even announced his intention to stay at the hotel. That was just another part of his strategy, she realised now, and was a reminder of the incisive mind behind the devastatingly handsome face. He made sure he was always the innocent party, the considerate party, the only one who always put Francesca first...

He must have rung the lawyer at home, Kate realised as the meeting drew to a close. Like everything else in his life, Santino Rossi had lawyers at his beck and call twenty-four hours a day. Such was the power of the man who had ranged himself against her, and she would do well to remember it. As far as Santino was concerned Francesca was the ultimate prize and even this meeting was just one more example to a sympathetic judge of his willingness to compromise and support the wayward single mother of his child.

The moment the meeting ended Kate went to find a quiet place where she could study in private the documents the lawyer had given her. She had been left with the nagging suspicion that by doing what she thought was best for Francesca she had compromised her position. She wasn't weak and she wasn't foolish, and she would fight for Francesca's right to know both her parents, but Santino was ruthless and made a formidable enemy, one she didn't possess the weapons to fight. Today's meeting was about compromise, the lawyer had told her, but compromise was a tool Santino only ever wielded for his own benefit. He looked further than today's battle and saw victory in a succession of cleverly constructed moves. She was just a pawn on his chessboard and unless she found a way to touch him before they reached a court of law she wouldn't stand a chance.

Finding a door partially open off the hallway, Kate slipped inside. Sitting tensely on the edge of a sofa, she scanned each page trying to make sense of the legalese. The dates were clear enough, and as she made a quick calculation of the days when each of them would have Francesca she thought the visitation rights seemed quite reasonable. Pausing a moment, she mulled it over. Maybe Santino was right and she was overreacting... She wanted to believe that. She wanted to believe that things wouldn't turn out to be as bad as she had feared...

Her gaze wandered to the window and her heart gave a ragged thump as she saw Francesca and Santino. They were just coming back to shore in a small rowing boat, the light wind ruffling Francesca's curls and doing the same to her father's thick black hair...

Kate looked away squeezing her eyes shut. *She still loved him.* She loved him so much that whatever Santino did to her she would always love him. Francesca was her life, but so was Santino...while in his life, she was nothing.

But she wouldn't hide in the house. Was that what he expected? That she would leave her meeting with the lawyer with her head bowed and her spirit broken. Standing up, Kate firmed her jaw. Her little girl was laughing in the sunshine and that was where she wanted to be...outside in the fresh air with Francesca. Picking up her bag, Kate stuffed the documents inside. She would have to look at them more closely another time.

By the time Kate reached the lakeside Santino was just lifting Francesca from the boat and setting her down on the wooden pier that jutted out in the lake. The moment she saw Kate, Francesca came flying across the grass to greet her. Capturing Francesca's momentum, Kate swung her high into the air. Francesca was bursting with excitement from everything she'd seen, including the island where she would be able to play pirates once she was older and had learned to sail...

Santino would be able to teach Francesca so many things, Kate reflected, smiling as she listened to the endless list of discoveries Francesca had made. If her daughter was happy she was happy—wasn't that how it had always worked in the past?

Kate had to stamp on the longing that threatened to overwhelm her when Santino walked up to them. She couldn't bear to look at him. She couldn't bear to see the expression of loathing on his face when he stared back at her. Her heart was so badly bruised she wasn't ready for another knock yet.

'Did your meeting go well?' His voice was clipped, but, as always, cleverly pitched in front of Francesca.

'Very well, thank you.' A glance at Francesca reassured Kate that they were both successful in keeping their true feelings from her.

'Good,' Santino said with satisfaction.

Kate flashed him a look over Francesca's head to let him know she was aware of all the risks she had run by falling in with his plan. The papers his lawyer had given her weighed heavily in her bag. Her secret hoard of misery, Kate thought bitterly, knowing there could be no going back. The legal machine was up and running, and as far as Santino was concerned the end of the journey was a foregone conclusion.

'Come along,' Francesca prompted, reaching for Kate's hand, 'We're going to have ice cream. *Gelato,*' she added, pronouncing the new word proudly and distinctly.

'Clever girl.' Kate forced a smile, knowing this was the first of many new Italian words Francesca would soon be speaking.

'You like ice cream, don't you?' Francesca pressed hopefully.

'Yes…but Daddy wants to have some time alone with you,' Kate explained as gently as she could. 'You and I have lots of opportunities to eat ice cream together, Francesca.' With every word Kate felt as if she were twisting a knife in her heart and Francesca's tears of disappointment gave it an added twist. However hard she tried not to, she was in danger of spoiling Francesca's day. She should have forgotten about putting on a brave show and stayed in the house out of the way.

'There's enough ice cream for everyone.'

Santino's remark was to forestall any emotional blunder, Kate realised. He could always read her so accurately and knew she was on the brink. For once, she could only be grateful to him. The last thing she wanted to do was break down in front of Francesca.

It pierced Kate's heart when Francesca smiled up at both of them, totally unaware of the deception they were playing out.

'Don't worry about me.' Kate's steady glance assured Santino that she was back under control. 'I'll have some ice cream with you another time, Francesca. I've got some things I must do.' She turned to go and kept on smiling, but she hated it, she hated any form of deception where Francesca was concerned.

But Francesca wouldn't take no for an answer and seized

her hand. And then she took Santino's hand so the three of them were linked.

She had to keep up the act, Kate told herself firmly. If Santino could do it, then so could she. But all the resolve in the world couldn't ease the pain of a broken heart. She had wanted so much more than this.

Meredith was waiting for them on the raised patio. Standing beside an old-fashioned ice cream cart, she was waving a child-sized apron like a flag. Kate felt anger flood through her at the thought that this was how Francesca's life was going to be from now on. What was wrong with a dish of ice cream, or an ice cream cornet, for goodness' sake?

She had calmed down a little by the time Francesca had served them all beautifully, but Kate still couldn't bring herself to meet Santino's eyes. She couldn't bear to see the adoration in his gaze when he stared at Francesca turn to cold contempt each time he looked at her.

There were heaters positioned on the patio to protect them from the slightest chill, but even so Kate shivered as she thought about her meeting with his lawyer and what it signified. Surely a child belonged with her mother? She had to believe that. She had to believe that any court would uphold that right…

'Kate, a word, please…'

Kate jolted back to attention as Santino spoke to her and saw he was standing, waiting for her to go with him. What now? What demands, what threats, would he put in place? But even as she shrank from the prospect of more power play she yearned to be with him, to be close to him, to have the opportunity to try and reach beyond the coldness and find his heart.

Thanking Francesca for his ice cream, he promised to visit her stall again very soon, and then turned to make sure Kate was following him.

Kate was so eaten up by anxiety on her way back into the house that she almost stumbled. Santino was there to catch her. He steadied her, his touch on her arm a poignant reminder of the old intimacy between them.

Her heart was always ready to take him back, Kate realised, but she had to stop wasting time on hopeless day-dreams and concentrate on securing the best possible outcome for Francesca.

'Do you think Francesca is happy?'

They had taken up positions on opposite sides of Santino's study and were facing each other.

'Of course,' Kate told him honestly. 'Anyone can see how happy she is…' Even as she spoke Kate was conscious that any innocent remark might work against her. Just by telling the truth she made it sound as if she were endorsing Santino's desire to keep Francesca with him in Rome. She would have to be on guard every moment and watch every word she said.

'And what do you think of my proposals regarding visitation rights? Do you think them fair?'

Fair… The word thundered in Kate's head, taunting her with what might have been, reminding her that now it all came down to a balancing act between them as they ensured Francesca's time was divided between them. 'Yes,' she said uncertainly, wishing now that she had stayed longer in the house to study the documents. The urge to be with Francesca had overwhelmed her and made her careless, and now she realised that it might have cost her dear. 'They seemed fair.'

'That's good. We need to get everything organised as quickly as possible to lessen the impact on Francesca.'

Lessen the impact on Francesca? Kate couldn't find any words in answer to that. Was Santino serious? How would a speedy decision lessen the impact on Francesca? Had he thought how this new regime would impact on her? How could it affect Francesca other than negatively when it took away from her everything she knew, everything she was comfortable with, everything in her innocence she believed would go on for ever? Santino might have convinced himself that a straightforward transaction could take place between them, but all the riches in the world couldn't reassure a child who had been uprooted from her home.

She almost felt sad for him as she looked at him. There was such confidence in his gaze, he was so sure he was right, whereas she felt as if a deep, dark pit had opened up and was waiting to claim her. She had held herself aloof for so many years only to fall in love with a man who didn't want her, a man whose arrant certainty threatened Francesca's happiness and who appeared at this moment to despise Kate to the point where he wouldn't be satisfied until he had destroyed her.

'Do you think yourself a fit mother, Kate?'

'Of course I do.' What did he mean? What sort of confession was he waiting for her to make?

'Really?'

Santino's voice surprised her. It had turned soft and seductive, and took her off her guard. When he came across the room she wasn't quick enough to evade him, or perhaps she didn't want to. The yearning inside her was certainly too great to resist him and when he took hold of her arms she was pliant in his grasp.

The clock ticked as her head rolled back allowing him to drop a kiss on the exposed tender flesh on her neck. She wanted so much to believe that everything would be all right, and that he had taken pity on her... The touch of his lips quickly enflamed her senses, raising her nipples, and causing something heavy to twist deep inside her.

'More?' he murmured softly.

She could only sigh and then that sigh became a moan.

Taking his cue, Santino rasped the rough stubble on his cheeks against Kate's tender neck.

'Kiss me, Santino…' The words came out on a breath and her eyes were barely focused. If only he would kiss her and hold her she knew that she had hope… She could see that his eyes were half shut and his lips were tugging up at one corner in a sexy, sardonic smile. The softening in his jaw was irresistible and he was gazing down at her in that sleepy, confident way he had…'Please…' Her hands crept up the sleeves of his lightweight jacket, and, growing in confidence, she sought the hard, tanned flesh beneath the open buttons on his shirt. 'Kiss me, Santino…' Her voice had grown stronger and more confident, and her hands were more demanding as they moved behind his neck so she could lace her fingers through his hair.

He made a pass with his lips that left her weak, and then his arms swept round her, bearing her weight. It was everything she had hoped for, more… On a sensory level she was floating, and on every other level Kate knew she was drawing closer to her goal to touch Santino's heart…

He let her drop and stood back.

'It's that easy, isn't it?' he said. 'You're that easy. If you think for one moment I would allow you to have custody of my daughter, you're mad. Do you really think that I would allow Francesca's innocence to be polluted by a *mother* like you?'

With a sound of disgust he left the room.

Kate remained where she was for quite some time…listening to the clock ticking on the wall, studying the tiny fibres in the carpet beneath her motionless limbs. She couldn't think; she didn't dare to. But eventually, like some animal returning from a deep sleep, she uncurled herself and rallied.

Because she had to, because she couldn't give up. However hopeless, however weary, this was one fight she could never turn her back on. She had to seek Santino out now and leave him in no doubt that, whatever had happened between them, she would contest any unreasonable suggestion he might make regarding Francesca's future. She would not be defeated, not where her child was concerned.

She found him in the sitting room, relaxing, reading the paper as if nothing untoward had happened. His brow creased as she walked into the room and then he studied her face for a moment over the top of the newspaper. Finding her recovered, he continued on with his reading as if she weren't there. But Kate noticed a tension had crept into his jaw. He had not expected her to recover so quickly, or perhaps at all.

In spite of his rudeness her heart raced as it always did at the sight of him. It was insane, it made no sense, but still she loved him, nothing would ever change where that was concerned. And at least Francesca had the father she had always longed for, Kate reminded herself, standing her ground. 'I just wanted to confirm that I will be consulting a solicitor as soon as we return to England...' Her throat felt tight, but somehow she managed to sound businesslike.

Santino took an inordinate amount of time lowering his paper. As he put it to one side Kate felt dread creeping over her. 'You wouldn't stop us leaving Rome?' she said, voicing her deepest fear.

'You? No.'

'What do you mean?' She felt the blood drain from her face.

'I would have thought that was obvious.'

Santino stood up. All the better to intimidate her, Kate thought as he towered over her.

'Francesca will be staying here in Rome with me.'

'No. I won't leave her.' Kate found some steel for her voice. Santino was merciless, she couldn't afford to appear weak.

He made an impatient gesture with his hand. 'This show of emotion helps no one, least of all Francesca. It's clear you haven't read the documents through, or you would know the dates I have proposed for my daughter's visits to Rome. They are clearly laid out. As Francesca is here in Rome it makes perfect sense for her to remain—'

'Perfect sense?' Kate interrupted him. 'To whom?'

Santino ignored her. 'For Francesca to remain here and grow accustomed to her new life.'

He said the words clearly and deliberately as if Kate had remained silent the whole time. 'Francesca already has a life with me.'

'And now that life will change to accommodate me.'

Swallowing back her fear, Kate struggled to remain calm. 'So you have made all the decisions regarding Francesca's future without consulting me?'

'You have just had a meeting with my lawyer. How much more considerate do you expect me to be?'

Yes, she could see that meeting would look good for him in a court of law.

'You had all the time in the world to ask him questions,' Santino pointed out.

'And I did ask him questions, about many things, but I was upset, and confused—'

'Excuses now?'

Kate shook her head at Santino's accusation, but it was true she had been distraught and not thinking straight. Kate Mulhoon, the one person everyone else relied on for clear direction, had gone to pieces in the only meeting of her life that really mattered.

'I've no time for this. If you had read the document through you would know the dates—'

'If I'd read the document?' Kate exclaimed. 'We're talking about our daughter, Santino, not a piece of paper. Do you really think Francesca's life can be divided into segments like an orange?'

'A court of law will make the final decision.'

'And you're happy to allow a judge who doesn't know Francesca to rule on what will or will not make her happy?'

'I'm not happy leaving that decision in the hands of Francesca's mother.'

'Then I'll see you in court, Santino.' But as Kate turned for the door he stood in her way.

'If you try to fight me you will regret it; I promise you that.'

'Are you threatening me?' Kate stared up into eyes that held no warmth for her and flinched when they sparked with amusement.

'I suggest you get a grip, Kate, or a court of law might consider you unstable, and judge you to be an unfit mother.'

'And I suggest you find someone else to bully, Santino, because where Francesca is concerned I will not allow you to intimidate me. Now please move away from the door.'

'With pleasure,' he said, opening it wide for her.

Kate stopped on the threshold. 'I can't believe I thought I was in love with you. What a lucky escape I've had.'

His gaze flickered and then turned cold again. 'And I thought you might have been different to other women. I even thought we might have had a chance—'

'You threw it away, Santino, and I only hope you don't pass on this hard, unyielding side of your nature to our daughter.'

'Have you finished?' He stared over her head.

'No.' Kate firmed her jaw. 'You should know that I will

abide by any ruling the court makes, but I won't be ruled by you, Santino, and I won't allow you to rule Francesca. We're both leaving Rome this weekend and the only way you can stop me taking her back home is by locking us up.'

'Don't be so dramatic.'

'No, I can see that might look bad for you. I don't imagine it's the kind of publicity you would relish.'

'Are you attempting to blackmail me?'

'I don't think you have the slightest idea the lengths a mother will go to in order to protect her child.'

'Get out! Just get out of my sight!'

Kate shuddered as the door slammed behind her.

The only thing keeping her together was Francesca and Kate rushed to see her now. After the terrible things she and Santino had said to each other she needed reassurance that Francesca was unaware of the enmity between her parents.

Kate found Meredith and Francesca in the garden, and as soon as Francesca spotted her she came running over, eager to show off the puppies to her mother.

It would be hard for Francesca to leave the puppies behind, Kate thought as the tiny animals raced around tumbling over each other in their excitement. *But not impossible.* She would find a way…perhaps Meredith wouldn't mind taking in another dog…

Francesca was happy to play on the grass while Kate went to sit on the terrace with Meredith beneath the bleached linen umbrella. Resting her chin on her hand, Kate watched Francesca and tried at the same time to close her mind to Santino. But she had only been sitting there a few minutes when he came out of the house. She could feel him behind her, but she would not let him spoil this innocent moment of enjoyment, Kate decided as his shadow moved across her.

She smiled and waved at Francesca. If Kate had needed anything to convince her that she could face whatever the future held, Francesca was enough; Francesca gave her all the courage she needed to go on.

The day had mellowed into the type of afternoon when nothing bad should ever happen, and apart from the tension between Santino and herself Kate might have believed it possible. Turning her face up to the flawless sky, she shut him out. 'It's so lovely here…' She waited for Meredith to reply and when only silence greeted her she opened her eyes to find she was alone with Santino.

'Meredith has taken Francesca inside.'

'Why?' Shading her eyes, Kate looked at him.

'For a rest before dinner, I believe.'

'Before dinner?

'My suggestion to Meredith was that you all stay the night. We will eat at six o'clock to accommodate Francesca's earlier mealtime.'

It was another decision taken out of her hands. As she fought to keep everything on an even keel for Francesca's sake she was in danger of being swept along at Santino's pace and in the direction he decided. But it was a long drive back to Rome and all the travelling had exhausted Francesca, another journey on top of the rest wasn't fair to her…

The moment Kate gave her agreement to his plan Santino stood up and walked away. Her sense of isolation deepened as she watched him returning to the house. Leaving the table, she hurried in the same direction. She could see Meredith and Francesca lingering for a few last moments with the puppies before returning inside. But her step faltered when she saw

Francesca throw herself into Santino's arms. As he lifted their daughter high in the air Kate felt tears sting her eyes. They were tears of happiness for Francesca, and tears of sadness because she would never be part of Francesca's new life. Not wanting to intrude, Kate paused and stared around at the fabulous grounds. How could she deny Francesca a heritage like this?

Santino had planned for their rooms to look over the stables. In fact the suite the maid showed Meredith, Kate and Francesca into was so spacious it overlooked both the stables and the lake. Francesca could hardly contain her excitement, which was understandable; she had never been anywhere quite so grand in her life.

Watching Francesca exploring their new quarters, Kate's first thought was that her daughter was going to be ruined. Her worst fears were only confirmed when she looked out of the window. Santino was in the stable yard holding a pretty white pony on a leading rein.

Biting her lip, Kate turned away. All Francesca had ever dreamed about was owning a pony of her own. Would she come back to England willingly now? It was the ice-cream cart all over again. Everything here was to excess… But then Santino was the master when it came to cutting deals, Kate remembered. Wasn't that what he was doing now? He knew that all he had to do was find the right currency and he could buy Francesca.

Kate took a few deep breaths until the panic inside her subsided. She had thought herself ready for anything, but she hadn't expected Santino to move so fast to secure Francesca. But wouldn't she do the same? Wasn't Santino in turmoil too? Shouldn't she be glad he was determined to assume his parenting responsibilities for Francesca? And Santino was new to this. She had a head's start on him…

But however hard she tried to convince herself that every-thing was working out for the best, Kate could never forget what she stood to lose. As Santino glanced up she moved back from the window. It was as if he knew she was standing there, watching him...

Then Francesca came tearing out of the bedroom with Meredith hot on her heels.

'Can we go down and see the pony?'

'Why not?' Kate gave Meredith a reassuring glance. Her aunt hadn't been so upbeat recently and Kate didn't want to spoil the day for Meredith either. They were here and she would smile and make the best of it. This was the beginning of a new chapter for all of them.

When they reached the stable yard it wasn't as easy as Kate had imagined to maintain a calm front, but she made it, standing quietly to one side while Francesca gazed in awe at the adorable shaggy white pony.

'Is he mine, Daddy?'

She was losing her. Kate felt as if she were holding onto sanity by her fingertips. She was *not* losing Francesca, Kate told herself firmly. They were looking at a pony in a stable yard, and that was all.

'The pony's name is Beppo,' Santino revealed.

When Santino smiled her heart thundered on cue, and she had to remind herself that his smile was not for her, but Francesca. And when she had done that it was her turn to smile and exclaim with pleasure and do all the things that Francesca expected of her, because that was the right thing to do. And the right thing was never easy.

'I'd like a pony,' Francesca hinted, glancing up at her father.

'A pony like Beppo?' Santino grew thoughtful.

'Yes.' Francesca was thrilled that her hint appeared to be reaping dividends. Unable to hide her triumph she glanced at Kate and then locked eyes with her father. 'Does Beppo live here?'

'He's considering it,' Santino admitted.

Kate could tell Francesca was having difficulty holding her excitement in check, and knew it was only moments before Santino closed the deal of his life.

'You say you'd like a pony like Beppo, Francesca,' he said, 'but could you take care of him?'

'I could learn,' Francesca said, growing serious as she looked up at her father.

'A pony takes a lot of looking after. He must have fresh food and clean water every day, and his stable needs cleaning out. He also needs a lot of grooming.'

Francesca's face fell as she considered the obstacles. 'Could I have a stool to stand on and someone to show me how?'

'Maybe it could be arranged…but only if your mother agrees.'

Kate couldn't have been more surprised, and was given no time to recover before he added, 'Even then Beppo wouldn't be your pony until I was convinced you could care for him properly, Francesca. And when you were in England you would have to find someone to look after him while you were away. And if you *ever* neglected him—'

'Oh, I wouldn't,' Francesca promised him fervently. 'And Mummy will be here to tell me what to do so that would never happen.'

Francesca didn't notice the silence that followed her declaration, or the sadness in her mother's eyes.

'I think you and Beppo should get to know each other…' Santino handed the leading rein to Kate. Tipping his chin towards the tack room door, he said, 'Take your time so that both of you can get to know him. Then pass him over to my head stable lad who will want to check him over before we commit to buying him. I'll see you all at dinner.'

Was this just another ploy to win favour with a judge? Santino was gone before Kate had chance to work out what he might be hoping to accomplish and was still staring at his retreating back when Francesca shook her arm.

'Can we walk Beppo round the yard?'

'Yes, of course darling,' Kate murmured distractedly. Santino had made a conciliatory gesture towards her by bringing her into the decision-making process, but did that mean he had softened in any way? Was he less of a threat? Or was the pony merely another bargaining counter?

In many ways Santino had proved himself a decent man who would make a good father to Francesca. In others… Kate sighed. She had so wanted to believe that destiny had intended their paths to cross and that there was purpose in it. But that purpose was Francesca, and only Francesca. It was enough. It was more than enough.

As she watched Francesca handling Beppo Kate had to admit that Santino's approach with the pony had been better than the ice cream, so maybe even he was learning. He hadn't made it easy for Francesca. If she wanted to own a pony like Beppo, Santino had made it clear that Francesca would have to earn the right…

'Sighing, Kate?' Meredith probed gently.

Kate turned to her aunt. 'When everything's been broken into little pieces, Meredith, can it ever be mended?'

'Yes, of course it can, if all the pieces can be found,' Meredith said with her usual common-sense slant.

But Meredith was the eternal optimist.

CHAPTER THIRTEEN

'DO YOU love Daddy?'

If Kate could have chosen one question to be barred from the dinner table that would have been it. Fortunately Santino had chosen that moment to lean away to ask one of his staff for something. 'Yes, I do,' she told Francesca honestly.

'So can we stay here and you will teach me how to look after the pony?'

'I'm sure Daddy will want to do that.' Kate's throat tightened as Francesca looked at her. This was how it started... with tiny lies. However hard she fought to build her life with Francesca on truth, she would have to fudge issues from now on to protect Francesca from being hurt.

'Can't you both teach me?' Francesca pressed.

'That won't be possible,' Kate explained, 'because you and I are returning to England this weekend, and the next time you come here you'll be on your own with Daddy.'

'No.' Francesca shook her head. 'You have to come too. And so does Gran Meredith.'

Kate's thoughts wavered unhappily about how much to tell Francesca; the last thing she wanted was a scene.

'What's the problem?' Santino turned to look at her.

'Your father knows more about horses than I do,' Kate said, thinking it politic to do so.

'You know everything,' Francesca argued stubbornly.

It was one of those moments when, had things been normal, they might have laughed, but Kate just felt torn. The tables had just turned in her favour, but she had no appetite for scoring some cheap point off Santino. As far as Francesca was concerned, Santino was a dream father, but he was still a stranger to her, and however exciting her new surroundings Francesca didn't take to the idea of coming to Rome to spend time on her own with a father she didn't know. It was a turning point Santino could not have anticipated, Kate guessed, seeing his eyes cloud with disappointment.

'Would it help if I stayed a little longer?' The words might have come out of nowhere and Kate was almost as surprised by her offer as Santino clearly was. But she had no reason to hurry back to England now Francesca was in Rome with her, and Santino had given ground over the pony. She was only showing that she could be reasonable too, which was the right thing to do with a court battle looming.

'Go on,' Santino prompted, raising her pulse just by turning to look at her.

'My shadow at the office can cope without me,' Kate told him. 'I see no reason why Francesca and I can't stay on…if that's all right with you?' She held his gaze, letting him know that this was no climb down, but a common-sense decision to move things forward for Francesca's sake.

'Very well,' Santino agreed. 'If that will make Francesca happy, I'll tell my housekeeper you will be staying on.'

The coldness in his eyes was almost worse than his anger, Kate thought as Francesca shrieked with excitement, but it was too late now to change her mind.

Meredith chose that moment to get up from the table. 'I think we'll leave you two to sort out the details. It's time for Francesca to go to bed. Will you excuse us?' Meredith held out her hand to Francesca, and with everything turning her way Francesca seized hold of Meredith's hand without complaint.

Santino was on his feet in an instant to help Meredith with her chair. Kate took the opportunity to draw Francesca into her arms. 'I'll come by later to tuck you in.'

'With Daddy?'

Kate hesitated. This wasn't going to get any easier.

'Of course with Daddy,' Santino confirmed, confining his glance to Francesca's face.

She had to stay and look the enemy in the eyes, Kate decided when Meredith and Francesca had left the room. She would not have Santino imagining she was running away from him. 'I hope it isn't inconvenient for you if I stay on with Francesca?' she said, out of politeness and in an attempt to break the silence that had fallen over the room.

Convenient? It was everything he had ever wanted. This was the closest he had come to having a family of his own, but like some distorted image at a fairground his dream had turned ugly. Why was he surprised? When it came to family, ugliness was all he knew.

As Kate looked at him he wondered if the wound inside him would ever heal. And now there was another wound, only this time Kate was the cause of it. He barely blinked when she started backtracking on her offer to help out almost immediately.

'We can't stay long. I'm sure you understand that I must seek legal advice at the earliest opportunity.'

'Oh, I understand,' he assured her. 'Why don't you

choose someone now? I'll pay for them. I'll have a lawyer of your choice flown out here. A team of lawyers, if that's what you want.'

'Please don't let's start arguing again,' she said wearily, making it sound as if he were in the wrong. Women were so predictable. They gave with one hand and took away with the other.

He left her to gaze out across the grounds. They had always soothed him in the past. They reminded him of just how far he'd come. But today they failed and all he felt was anger and frustration. He would not lose his daughter. Not now he had found her. The only way he knew how to stave off the crippling fear of loss instilled in him as a child was to fight, to fight back, to *always* fight back…

'I said, thank you, Santino.'

He turned. 'Thank you for what?' he demanded brusquely.

'For offering to fly a lawyer over to Rome for me.'

But…? His lips curved with contempt. He could already hear the prevarication in her voice. She didn't want her lawyer here where they might be influenced by his obvious wealth and status.

'I don't want a lawyer to come here, and see all this,' she said.

Having his poor opinion of her confirmed was scant consolation, but his lips curved in a grim smile of acknowledgement just the same.

'They might think it's an opportunity to go for a ridiculous settlement in order to get their cut out of it.' Her gaze was level as she stared him down. 'And I think we both know that what's really at stake is Francesca's happiness.'

Not for the first time she had surprised him. She had taken his preconceptions and turned them on their head. It should have pleased him to think Francesca's mother had such foresight as well as such consideration for his fortune, but in his present mood he didn't feel like cutting Kate any slack. She had thrown him once with her offer to stay on, and now again with this shrewd observation, but that didn't mean he was anywhere near revising his opinion of her. 'Presumably you'd choose your lawyer with more care than that—'

She cut him off. 'Thank you for the offer, but I prefer to take my legal advice on neutral ground.'

He wasn't accustomed to people refusing the offers he made. He wasn't used to dissent of any kind. Kate was so stubborn and self-willed she reminded him of himself at times, but that didn't mean he had to trust her. It didn't mean he had to drive her away either. If he did that she might find some way to take Francesca with her and he couldn't risk it. He couldn't risk Francesca's happiness either, by parting her from her mother. 'I would make an office available to you. Any discussion you have would be completely private.'

'In England?' One finely drawn brow rose as she held his gaze.

He eased his neck. 'Do you have to be so difficult?'

'If you mean do I have to stand up for myself? Then yes, Santino, I do,' she told him frankly.

Kate was determined not to show any sign of weakness. She knew the type of future she had with Francesca depended on how she conducted herself in front of Santino now. 'One week, Santino…' Her voice was calm. She wanted to avoid confrontation at all costs. They had reached a plateau where at least they could be civil with each other, and she had to keep that line of communication open for as long as she could. 'One week and then Francesca and I must go home.'

'To England?'

His face had changed. Something wasn't right. A ripple of

fear ran down Kate's spine as she held Santino's gaze. 'Yes, of course to England.'

'You'd better think again,' he said in a voice turned hard. 'My daughter isn't going anywhere until my rights as her father are secured.'

'Your rights?' Kate could hardly breathe for all the terror inside her, but her eyes turned steely. 'What about our daughter's rights?'

'Yes, what about them, Kate? Francesca should be aware of all the opportunities open to her, don't you think?'

'Do you imagine Francesca is for sale to the highest bidder?'

'I hope you know that's not the way I think.'

She did, and it had been a cheap shot, Kate acknowledged, but she was desperate. In Rome she had no contacts, no influence, and she knew the battle to reclaim a tug-of-love child could turn into a long-drawn out process and that was the last thing she wanted for Francesca.

'What if your lawyer drew up a contract stating that I grant you full access to Francesca until this can be properly settled in a court of law? Would that reassure you?' She was offering him an olive branch, but could tell right away that Santino wasn't open to any suggestion other than his own. 'I'll sign it and you can have it witnessed, and then your rights will be secured.' He made no response. 'Francesca must come home with me,' Kate stressed firmly. 'There can be no ambiguity where that is concerned.'

As Santino continued to study her face Kate pressed on. 'Surely you agree that the best way to reassure Francesca is to keep things amicable between us? And you would have a contract,' she pointed out, hoping that talk of a contract would reassure Santino more than any promises she could make.

'Very well,' he said at last.

'Thank you.' Kate could hardly hide her relief as Santino walked away. But what had she agreed to? Another week of dancing round lawyers, of fighting tooth and nail for Francesca, of trying to avoid Santino finding reason to call her emotional state into question? Another week with no guarantees that at the end of it Santino would allow Francesca to leave Rome?

She was shaking by the time she followed Santino inside the house. Her nerves were shot. She felt as if they were standing on opposite sides of a huge divide yelling demands at each other, while Francesca was down in the crater being ignored by both of them. And very soon she would have to tell Francesca the truth about her parents' relationship. If she left it too long Francesca would end up hurt and bewildered, and would grow up to have the same lack of trust imbedded in her as Santino, which was the last thing Kate wanted. She had no option but to go to Santino one last time and ask him if they could form a united front to tell Francesca how things stood between them. If Francesca heard it from both of them it would be easier for her to accept. And once that was done both of them should put all talk of contracts and lawyers aside and spend the rest of their time in Rome smoothing Francesca's path into her new life.

He was both surprised and irritated when he called out in answer to the knock on his study door and Kate walked in. He had shut himself away to consider his strategy and prowled deeper into the shadows now so she couldn't see his face. He hadn't wanted the full light of day and had closed the shutters, seeking darkness to lick his wounds like a creature of the night. His wounds had not come from any loss of ground where Francesca was concerned, but from his continuing attraction to Kate, a woman who had lied and cheated him out of the first five years of Francesca's life. He wanted to get over it—get over her, like an illness. She had wounded him, she had torn out his heart, but he still wanted her. How could that be possible?

'I want to talk to you about Francesca.'

'You'd better come in and shut the door,' he said, turning to open the shutters. He had to confess it had taken courage for her to seek him out. He could hear the nervousness in her voice like an undertone in a complex chord. 'What do you want, Kate? Haven't we said all we have to say to each other?'

'I can never say enough where Francesca's concerned.'

'Your piety is beginning to get me down—if only because it's such a sham.'

She made a helpless gesture with her arms. 'You must believe what you will of me.'

'What do you hope to gain by seeking me out like this?'

'For me? Nothing,' she said.

He refused to look at her directly, but in his peripheral vision he could see the sunbeams sifting through the slatted blinds had sprinkled her hair with gold. 'I'm listening.' He turned his head and stared straight at her.

'We must show a united front to Francesca. We must go to her and tell her what's happening—'

He cut across her. 'Sit down.' She couldn't just come in and issue orders as she had on the film set. Who did she think she was? He took his usual place on the opposite side of the desk, keeping things formal between them. There would be no cosy family get-togethers here.

'My staying on in Rome will make it easier for you to get to know Francesca.'

'That's very considerate of you.'

'I have no wish to make things any harder for you.'

No, but he couldn't help thinking she had learned from him and was building a case. What this was really about was telling him Francesca would never be happy in Rome without her mother at her side.

'I don't want to argue with you, Santino—'

'I'm sure you don't. You came here to persuade me to do as you wish.' He paused. She looked uncomfortable. 'Well, let me tell you, I'm happy to leave everything to the lawyers.'

'Can't we at least keep this civilised?'

'Of course,' he confirmed readily. 'That's what lawyers are for.'

She held his gaze for a moment and then, realising it was a lost cause, she stood up.

He didn't know what was annoying him more—the fact that she was going, or the fact that he wanted to call her back. He still wanted her, and there was that connection between them that neither of them knew how to break. That same bond was keeping her at the door when she should have gone by now.

As she turned to look at him he felt the unmistakable tug of sexual attraction. It never wavered or diminished, and even in the midst of such upheaval it was like a third force joining them in the room. Her eyes were growing dark, and her full chiselled lips were damp where she had nervously moistened them with her tongue. The longer he stared at her, the more he longed for comfort and release. He eased his shoulders, hoping that would help, and closed his eyes to fight off the images of her naked. All he wanted was oblivion and a break from all the painful memories…

But his mind was full of Kate, and all he could think was that her nipples would be tight pink buds by now. Even at eighteen her breasts had felt heavy in his hands…heavy and silky soft. He could remember her slender limbs creaming into compliance, and her thighs, moon-pale and satin-smooth beneath his touch leading him on to the warm, dark secrets of her body. Was she swollen and throbbing for him now? Did she ache for him as much as he ached for her? They could find relief in each other's arms…'You shouldn't have come here, Kate.'

The words rippled through her body like a song. But it was a song with words Kate knew she must close her ears to. Santino's eyes were dark and compelling, and glowed with a fire that promised to warm her through, and she needed to feel warm again so badly. Closing her eyes, she tried to hang onto the moment before she left the room so she could remember how his eyes grew slumberous when he wanted her. And as she parted her lips to suck in air she remembered how it felt when Santino kissed her…

'Don't let me keep you.'

His gaze had been heated, but now his voice was cold. Santino had been playing her like a cat with a mouse he intended to eat, Kate realised. Having thrown an erotic noose around her and drawn it tight, he had released it again just to prove that he could.

She had to be strong and fight this attraction. She had to school herself to feel nothing for him. She had to close her heart and mind to him. She had to grow numb and feel nothing, until whatever Santino said or did couldn't hurt her any more.

CHAPTER FOURTEEN

IT WAS only after he had tucked Francesca up in bed that Santino finally had chance to confront his demons. He went for a long walk around the grounds thinking about Kate and how he felt it necessary to prove she had no power over him. He had to know that no woman could ever hurt him again.

Anger had been his constant companion since childhood, and that anger had only redoubled when he had first learned about Francesca. His mind had been filled with thoughts of revenge. But it was hard to sustain such destructive emotions when he only had to think about the look in his daughter's eyes to know that Francesca's innocent hope was that he would be the father she had always longed for. Unwittingly, Francesca was doing her best to prove that the power of love was absolute, and now he was finding that the protective circle he had drawn around his life was under threat from the love of a child.

He'd had hours since then to contemplate the wretched mess he'd made of his life…time to think about an innocent girl with a disapproving family, a girl who had been left frightened and alone to cope with a pregnancy, but who had bravely decided to keep the baby. He couldn't imagine what might have happened if Kate hadn't had her aunt Meredith.

At that point his stomach had twisted in a knot, or was that his heart? He only knew that a world without Francesca was something he wasn't prepared to contemplate.

Kate and he were the same. Effectively she had been abandoned too, but like him, had made it through. Kate had made Francesca the centre of her world, and had passed on her courage to his daughter. That was why Francesca was so happy, a fact he had chosen not to recognise up to now. But that didn't mean he wouldn't do everything in his power to take Francesca from Kate.

Kate had tried and failed to put Santino out of her mind. She had tried to be strong and fight the attraction she felt for him and had only succeeded in remembering the pleasure he could bring her with the lightest brush of his lips or touch of his hands. She couldn't sleep, she couldn't rest, she could only pace the room and yearn to be with him, to be close to him, to share the closest intimacy of all. She had nothing to lose. He had hurt her so many times there wasn't anything left for him to bruise.

That was how she felt as she closed the bedroom door carefully behind her and padded silently in bare feet across the deeply carpeted landing to his room. And that was how she felt when she opened the door to Santino's bedroom and walked inside.

She came to him in silence, slipping beneath the sheets, her hands and mouth seeking him, finding him…

'Kate?' He was half asleep. His voice was lazy, his limbs were lazy, but his libido was firing on all cylinders. She had chosen her moment in a masterly fashion in a way that even he would have been proud of. His defences were down and likely to remain so for quite some time. He eased into her like coming home and would have paused to savour the moment, but her hunger was at fever pitch and she had plans for him.

She fell on him, kissing him with all the ferocity he knew she had always had locked inside her. He made it on top, swinging her beneath him, pinning her down. There were no words between them, only gasps and sharp urging cries as she came for a first time and then very quickly a second.

'Now…now,' she begged him hoarsely, raking his shoulders with her fingernails as she opened herself more for him. 'Give me more…'

It seemed she couldn't get enough of him as she bucked and strained, shamelessly positioning herself with her hips held high to achieve maximum penetration. Drawing back her knees, she thrust up her hips, claiming him, claiming all of him. She was seeking oblivion, a constant state of oblivion, just as he was. The first thrust inside her had been a hot, melting journey of temptation, and with her legs locked around his waist he had no doubt that in this at least he was her slave.

'More, more, Santino,' she cried out, her fingers biting cruelly into his shoulders. Her teeth raked him as he worked, and her tongue laved him, pressing him to move faster, thrust deeper, and move firmly against her as she rose up to meet him. She came quickly again, selfishly, monumentally, crying out as a seemingly endless succession of powerful waves claimed her. And as her muscles spasms gripped him he found his own powerful release, claiming her, joining her, until at last they lay panting and spent in each other's arms.

He felt replete and content, and even relaxed, perhaps for the first time in ages, certainly since she had come back into his life, while Kate murmured like a contented pussycat, settling herself comfortably in a series of sensual twists and turns, winding her legs around him until they were joined in a more innocent way than they had been previously.

'This doesn't change anything Kate,' he felt bound to warn her.

There was a pause, and then she whispered, 'I know that…'

He didn't believe her for a moment.

They woke again in the early hours of the morning in the lilac light before dawn. They had slept snuggled together like two halves of the same person, satiated and complete, but now as he twirled a lock of Kate's silky soft hair around his hand he found it such an easy matter to slide into her. She even angled herself for him though he wasn't certain that she was properly awake. But then she thrust her buttocks against him and he was sure.

It was almost too much pleasure rocking rhythmically in the silence knowing that she wanted him and that it was an emotion-free arrangement born of mutual sexual hunger, with no burdensome commitments on either side. When daylight came they would be enemies again, but now they were as close as two human beings could ever be. It was the biggest turn on he had ever known.

Her hair was short now but it still floated as she moved, catching the moonlight, which frosted it with silver. Her body was smooth beneath his hands and as he turned her onto her back the streaks of light pouring through the windows allowed him to enjoy her to the full…the lush curves, the lithe limbs, the surprisingly full breasts with the nipples drawn into tight hard buds. Pulling back for a moment, he enjoyed her cries of dismay. 'Do you want me still?' he murmured incredulously, wondering at her stamina.

'For ever,' she whispered.

The thought of the preparations her body was making to

receive him and the smooth, slick warmth that awaited him stole away the last of his control and with a sharp cry of satisfaction he sank into her again.

They slept again, but only for a short while and he was woken by her hand stroking his stubble-roughened cheek. He opened one eye and stared at her. 'What?'

'You're beautiful,' she said softly.

'That's my line,' he said dryly, reaching for her.

'Don't you want to sleep?' she teased him as he stroked the inside of her thigh.

'Do you?'

She groaned softly as his hand strayed, but recovered her composure when it didn't stray enough.

'What are you thinking?' she whispered, moving restlessly, wanting more of him.

'Whether you're really sufficiently recovered to start over…' Turning onto his back, he tormented her with the appearance of withdrawing his services.

'Try me…'

Turning, he lifted himself on one elbow and stared down into her face. 'No regrets?' He only asked because at that moment she seemed so vulnerable. Sometimes she was so strong, and yet at other times he knew she was at his mercy. And though it should have pleased him, he was discovering he had a conscience. Not much of one, admittedly, but enough to grant her the most basic human consideration.

'None,' she assured him, but he thought her eyes turned misty for a moment, but then she smiled and said with more bravado, 'No, none at all… And now I want more…' She moved shamelessly beneath him, offering him the delights of her body.

'First this…'

'What?' she said, clearly dismayed by any suggestion of delay.

'This,' he whispered, dipping his head to kiss her on the lips.

He had to taste her, he had to plunder this last bastion, and in some ways it seemed to him to be the greatest intimacy of all. And as he kissed her he felt a surge of emotion inside him that grew and grew as he deepened the kiss. It was like nothing he had ever known before and he didn't want it to end. So he finished it before he could be won over.

As he pulled away she was already arcing up to receive him. This was the insatiable lover he took such pleasure in. 'I'm happy to accommodate your demands…' He smiled against her mouth, teasing her in other places by touching and withdrawing. But then he was lost and groaned as she closed her muscles around him. It felt so good when she held him tightly. And then they moved in perfect harmony, easily and powerfully, like two lovers who had known each other for far more than one lifetime.

'Santino…'

As she breathed his name against his mouth in that excited way she had, he knew she was close and, kissing her deeply, he drank her ecstatic cries into his mouth. It had become important to him that she should experience more pleasure than she had ever known. He wanted her to lose control in his arms, as he needed to lose himself and forget. Only this time within moments of calming she was crying out and bucking wildly beneath him again so that he had to hold her in place to watch the pleasure unfolding on her face. 'You're very greedy,' he chastised her softly, still moving rhythmically inside her.

'No more…finished,' she panted, her mouth open to expose her pearl white teeth. But he proved her a liar by continuing to thrust, very gently at first, and then applying a little more pressure until her eyes widened and her fingers clawed in desperation at his shoulders.

'Yes…yes,' she gasped excitedly, 'You were right, Santino…I want more… Please, don't ever stop…'

In this situation he was only too happy to obey.

The sun had edged the drapes with gold when Kate was woken by Santino's kisses. He was torturing the very sensitive place below her ear and then the nape of her neck. And all the time his hands were teasing her and stroking her, at first firmly, and then lightly, until she was thrashing beneath him helpless with delight. But he would not touch the most sensitive place of all where, though she was still throbbing from his earlier attentions, he still wanted more. 'I want you, Santino. I want you again…'

'Not yet…' He smiled against her mouth. 'And not at all if you ask… No,' he warned huskily when she tried to guide him. 'I decide when.'

Kate yielded to the pleasure of delay. Santino had taught her that it only increased her hunger. But as he circled her straining nipples with his tongue and she looked down at the powerful spread of his shoulders, his tanned, smooth, muscular shoulders, she knew she couldn't wait.

'You are a witch,' he murmured, his lips curving with approval as she showed him what she wanted. 'You know I can't resist you…'

'Is there any reason why you should?' Locking her legs around his waist, she tempted him on. Lured by the silken promise of velvet steel cloaked in honeyed warmth, Santino took her again, moving firmly, and rhythmically, using fierce words of encouragement in his own language until Kate drew close to falling apart in his arms.

This was how he loved to see her, wild and abandoned and

passionate, with the walls of her citadel lying in ruins around her. Now there was only the Kate he wanted, the sweet Kate, the passionate Kate, the loving Kate… He could believe she was different from all other women when she came to him like this. He could believe she would be this way for ever. 'Let yourself go,' he urged her roughly.

And she did.

Kate woke later than Santino. She could hear him in the shower. She listened to him towelling dry, and then dressing, keeping her eyes shut all the time. She wanted to preserve the moment, the memories. They were so precious to her because they meant Santino had changed towards her. He had discovered what it was he really wanted…and he wanted her, he wanted a family, he wanted everything she wanted. It was like a miracle.

Snuggling deeper into his bed, Kate inhaled Santino's in-toxicating scent. This was her bed now, her bedroom, the bedroom she shared with Santino. She could already picture Francesca in an ivory silk dress with a sash and a net under-skirt, and with a coronet of fresh flowers on her hair. Perhaps they could find a pair of dainty cream ballet shoes for her feet. Francesca would make such a beautiful bridesmaid…

He dressed with care, leaving Kate asleep in bed. He didn't want to wake her. He didn't want to see the questions in her eyes. He wanted everything simple and clean-cut, like the contract he had drawn up and approved. And there was no reason on earth why he couldn't have it.

But she wasn't asleep and reached out to him, stretching her arm over the side of the bed, her hand feeling for him.

'What?' he said impatiently, checking the collar on his shirt in the mirror where he had just discovered that someone had forgotten to replace a button. There was a time for sex and there was a time for work and he had telephone calls that wouldn't wait.

'You're not leaving me?'

He was tempted to tell her he had never been with her, not in the sense Kate meant, but that would have been too harsh, even for him. 'I have things to do,' he said instead.

'Can't they wait?'

He had to stop himself exclaiming with incredulity. 'No,' he managed mildly, 'they can't wait.' And then, because he sensed some straight talking was in order, he turned to face her. 'Nothing's changed, Kate.'

She went pale as she stared at him. 'What do you mean?' she said faintly.

'I mean nothing's changed between us. The sex was good, but—'

'No.' She yelped the word, holding up her hand and jumping out of bed in the same moment. 'I don't want to hear—'

'I don't know what you imagined.'

'That's just it, isn't it, Santino?' Her eyes were blazing when she stared at him. 'I have an incredible imagination.'

He gave her a look as if to say he didn't know what she was talking about.

'For instance, I imagined we made love last night, whereas you have just pointed out we had sex. Silly me.'

He glanced at his watch. 'I don't have time for this, Kate.'

'No. You never have time for anything remotely awkward, do you, Santino?'

'If I had any idea what you were talking about…' He gave a typical Latin shrug.

'Don't let me keep you, Santino. I'm sure you have far more important things to do.'

'You can use my bathroom if you like. You'll find some clean towels on the heated rail, and—'

'You're too kind,' she cut across him acidly.

He didn't trouble to answer her.

When Kate went down for breakfast Santino was already chatting easily with Meredith and Francesca. Meredith's spoon froze halfway to her mouth as she waited to see how Kate and Santino would behave towards each other, while Francesca's expression became instantly wary.

How had she missed so much? Kate wondered. Had she been wearing blinkers? Had she forgotten so easily her concerns for Francesca's happiness? This was never going to work. She should never have come here. Francesca might only be a young child, but she was sensitive to what was going on between the people she loved.

Kate could only be relieved when shortly after she had joined them at the table Santino was called away to take a telephone call.

'Are you all right?' Meredith asked her softly. 'Did you tell him everything?'

Kate could hardly speak. The emotion inside her was so great her throat ached with the effort of keeping it in check. She realised at once that Meredith had mistaken her tired, pale appearance and devastated expression for grief after telling Santino everything he had a right to know. And in some ways Meredith was right, because she was grief-stricken, but only because she hadn't told Santino, and only because she was a fool to think he had changed towards her…to think he loved her.

Santino didn't love her, Kate accepted bitterly. Santino loved sex with her, and that would never, *never* be enough.

'You did talk to him?' Meredith pressed when Kate

remained silent. 'You did tell Santino everything?' Meredith's sunny face grew suddenly anxious.

Kate's hesitation said more than words ever could. She had never lied to Meredith.

'You didn't tell him, did you, Kate?'

Meredith sounded so disappointed Kate could hardly bear it, but as she reached across the table to reassure her aunt Santino came back into the room.

'Told me what?' he said. 'Kate?' he prompted when she remained silent. 'Will you excuse us?' he said pleasantly to Meredith, drawing Kate aside. 'Francesca,' he added when she ran after them. 'Please go with Meredith.'

'Why?'

'You can take Meredith down to the stables. I need to speak to your mother now.'

This time he made no pretence at gentleness when he referred to Kate, and Kate only had to see Francesca's face crumple to know that all her good work had been undone. Santino imagined he had overheard something confidential between herself and Meredith, and no doubt his suspicious mind was already conjuring up some nightmare scenario in which she played the role of the leading culprit. In many ways he was right, because they had been referring to a nightmare, but it wasn't the type of nightmare Santino imagined.

'Kate…'

His voice was harsh. She couldn't linger. She couldn't make this any worse for Francesca than it already was.

'Well?' Santino said the moment he closed the door of the study. 'Should I be concerned? Should I speak to Meredith?' he pressed when Kate remained silent.

'Don't bring Meredith into this.'

'Why not?' His dark eyes narrowed with suspicion.

'Because I'm asking you not to.'

'More secrets, Kate?' His hands tensed.

'It's not what you imagine.'

'How do you know what I imagine?'

'I can guess,' she said quietly. 'You always think the worst of me.'

'And you make it so easy for me to trust you?'

'There are some things I can't just blurt out.'

'Then tell me what it is you're hiding, or I will find out.'

'I can't change what you think about me, Santino. I can only promise you that I have a very good reason for holding back.'

'Holding back? Is that what you call it?'

Every inch of him was tense and she wanted so badly to reassure him, but what she had to say couldn't be said while he was so angry. Would a good time ever come? The grief was still so fierce, even after all this time.

'Well?' Santino pressed again. 'Are you determined to waste more of my time, or are you going to explain what this is about?'

A feeling of calm and certainty came over her. She had to tell him.

Kate reached for the silver locket she always wore around her neck, but just as she did so, irritated by the delay, Santino started for the door.

'This isn't going to work, Kate.'

'No…please…wait…'

'What? *What?*'

There was such hostility in his voice Kate's courage failed her. What she had to tell him couldn't be said into an atmosphere of aggression. But she had to say something or Santino would never listen to her again. 'When we're with Francesca please don't mention this difficulty between us…'

'And what do you suggest I do?' he demanded scathingly.

'Just don't mention the fact that there are formal arrangements for visits before we speak to her together and explain what's going on.'

'So instead we say she's going on holiday, or it's an exciting treat; a change from her usual routine?'

'Yes.'

She looked relieved.

'And if she asks why we don't live together?'

'That's easy…your business doesn't allow it.'

She paused to gauge his reaction.

'Anything else?' When it came to stirring his passions— all of them—Kate certainly had the inside track. This wasn't what she had been going to tell him. This was something she had thought up on the spur of the moment to avoid the truth. If he had been inclined to violence he might have felt like taking hold of her and shaking her. Instead he seethed inwardly, and pretty violently at that.

She tried sweet reason next, speaking to him in a voice that was low and beseeching while she used her beautiful soft grey eyes to implore him. 'Do we have to go to court, Santino, and expose Francesca to all the ugliness that will entail?'

'Of course we do. Until you start being honest with yourself how can you expect me to trust you?'

He heard her shocked intake of breath as he turned his face away. He suspected that whatever she was hiding was going to rattle them both when it finally came out.

'I *am* being honest with myself.'

'Are you, Kate?' It didn't surprise him to hear her voice was shaking. 'I don't think you are.'

'Please listen to me. I'm the mother of your child, Santino.'

That hit him on a raw nerve. 'The mother of my child who won't even tell the truth to Francesca?'

'I always tell Francesca the truth.'

'No. I tell Francesca the truth. What you're proposing is to tell her a sanitised version of the truth that you mistakenly think is going to help her. Francesca already knows there's something wrong between us, and if she hasn't figured it out yet, she soon will.'

'I'm only trying to protect her until we can speak to her together. Why can't you trust me?'

'Trust you?' His eyebrows rose. 'Why should I? And I'm not prepared to take any chances where Francesca's future is concerned.'

'Santino, please don't go—'

It was already too late. He was halfway through the door.

CHAPTER FIFTEEN

KATE caught up with Santino in the hallway, holding onto his sleeve when he tried to pull away.

'Stop it, Kate. This has gone far enough.'

'You have to believe me, Santino. I'm not hiding anything from you. At least, I am,' she tempered, hanging her head, 'but it's not what you think…' Her voice had sunk to a murmur.

'My daughter's waiting for me. Please step out of my way.' He was trying to be reasonable, but she really was testing his patience.

'All I'm asking is five minutes of your time.' She moved in front of him, blocking his way.

He shook his head incredulously. 'What do you want from me Kate? What is this? Another fantasy? Another pack of lies? Are you trying to make this little tragedy we're playing out more palatable?' With an impatient sound he wrenched his arm out of her grip.

'No!' Her voice had changed. It had become feral and fierce. She chased after him, springing in front of him, and the expression on her face would have been enough to stop anyone in their tracks.

'You will listen to me.'

'What is it?' He shook his head wearily, wondering if he could take any more. He was wound up tight as it was.

'Something that concerns both of us.'

The intensity of her gaze made him hesitate. 'Five minutes,' he conceded. 'We'll go to my study.'

He remained standing by the desk, toying with a pen, feeling awkward, wanting the interview to be over before it started. When he glanced up he found she wasn't looking at him. She was gazing out of the window and the light was illuminating her face as if she were waiting for her close up in a film. Playing the role of the tragic heroine, no doubt. But in truth to him she did look worn and drained.

As she turned to face him she made a helpless gesture with her hands. 'Now it comes to it I don't know where to start.'

'At the beginning?' he suggested. He was still feeling angry and suspicious, but something warned him not to push her too hard.

'It isn't easy…' She turned her face away from him to look out again across the lawn towards the lake. 'If I spend too much time thinking about it, I—'

'Stop thinking about it and tell me.' His voice was brusque. He wanted to provoke a reaction.

'I couldn't ever risk it ruling my life and so I shut it out. And now the guilt—'

She broke off and he could see tears trembling on her lashes. 'Go on,' he prompted with fractionally less ferocity.

'Francesca needs a mother who is strong and steady, not someone who breaks down in tears all the time…'

Was she admitting to some sort of mental frailty? Should he warn her that in her situation that was hardly wise?

'I wanted to be a mother she could have fun with, not someone who was always looking back and—'

'And what, Kate?' Pushing the pen away, he straightened up.

This was one of the hardest things she had ever had to do. Trying to find the right words made the blood drum in her head, and the throbbing behind her eyes was almost unbearable. She closed them now to shut out the light, the light that was threatening to intrude on the darkness inside her. She could hear Santino pouring water into a glass and even that sound splintered into a thousand cruel shards that pierced her memory, throwing her back in time to a day when she had been listening to the strident cries of a newborn child, and listening in vain for the sound of a second baby.

The look on her face frightened him. He hadn't been so much at a loss since he'd been six years old. The world had seemed a very big place to him then, and his part in it very small. He had that same feeling now. He felt dwarfed by the intensity of the grief on Kate's face.

He surprised himself. Hunkering down in front of her, he took her hands. 'You should talk about it…' Whatever *it* was.

She stared for a long time at her hands in his.

'I want to help you, Kate, but I can't if you won't tell me what's wrong.' He was brisk, businesslike. It was the only way he knew.

'I don't think you can help me,' she whispered.

His natural arrogance won through. 'I'm sure I can.'

Her answer was to open the locket at her neck.

'What is that?' He stared at the tiny black curl of silky hair and frowned.

'I lost your baby, Santino…'

He was falling fast into the same black hole Kate was in. 'But Francesca,' he managed before darkness closed over him.

'Was a twin. I lost your son, Santino. I lost our baby boy—'
He didn't hear any more.

She had lost a baby, their child, he understood her now and everything made sense—except his brutish behaviour towards her. *If he'd only known!* The words beat at his brain as he put his arms round her. It was like embracing a marble statue. For once he was lost, he didn't know what to do, he only knew that he wanted to get her walking, moving, living again. 'Shall we go outside…walk in the garden?' He didn't want her to be cooped up in a room where there was so much grief.

'I can't take the risk of Francesca seeing me like this…'

Her lips barely moved, she was barely functioning at a normal level, but even now her first consideration was Francesca.

'Why don't I take you to my apartment in Rome? Francesca is happy here with Meredith and we could have some time together…' If she said yes they could move forward; if she said no there was nowhere to go.

Dumbly, she nodded her head.

They drove back in silence to the centre of Rome where he kept an apartment in the fifteenth century Palazzo Doria Pamphilj. It was next to the official residence of the Italian Prime Minister and was his private citadel, his castle, his keep. He never invited anyone back. Ever.

The presence of black-suited security guards with receivers lodged discreetly in their ears and holsters concealed beneath their jackets appointed to protect Italy's most powerful politician ensured his privacy too, just the way he liked it.

A man he recognised acknowledged his return with the smallest flicker of his eyes. There was a longer, lingering stare for Kate, and not just because she was a fresh face. Though she hadn't spoken a word, let alone cry, her anguish was apparent, even to a stranger.

He led her inside the building and into the elevator, using a code and an electronic card both times to gain access. He wished the lift would travel faster so he could warm her frozen fingers and bring some expression back into her face, but he had to control his impatience; he couldn't risk doing anything that might alarm her. Nor could he chance revealing how he felt…the shock, the pain, the bewilderment… This was about Kate and the loss of her baby, the greatest wound a woman could sustain.

He brought her inside, whispering something out of her earshot to his housekeeper. Taking her into his study, where the light was kinder than the sitting room with its panoramic windows overlooking the Piazza Venezia, he led her to the couch in front of the crackling log fire and sat her down.

A discreet knock and a rustle of skirts heralded the arrival of his elderly housekeeper with a tray of hot milk and a plate of home-made biscuits. As he had asked she had brought a folded blanket with her, which she carried lodged beneath her arm. Without a word she put down the tray and then, leaving the blanket on the low table in front of the sofa where Kate was sitting, she left the room, closing the door quietly behind her.

'Kate…' He wasn't sure that she heard him. She was sitting in exactly the same position as she had when he carefully sat her down, but she had started to shiver. Unfolding the blanket, he wrapped it round her shoulders. Adding a shot of brandy to the steaming milk, he stirred in a spoonful of sugar before holding it to her lips. 'Drink this…'

She did so obediently like a child, taking small sips as he held the cup up to her mouth, but her eyes were blank and she didn't seem to be focusing on anything, least of all him. When her face finally pinked up he put the cup back on the tray and made a pillow for her head from the cushions. Lifting her legs one by one, he removed her footwear and arranged the blanket over her. Then, turning out the table lamp, he left her to sleep.

He made several phone calls and had almost paced a hole in the hall floor by the time he heard her stir. Returning to his study, he found her sitting up with her elbows on her knees and her head in her hands.

'Kate, don't cry. You're not alone any longer. We'll get through this together.'

'You won't forgive me,' she said with certainty. 'How can you ever forgive me?'

'Don't say that. There's nothing to forgive. I would rather ask how can I forgive myself for the way I treated you? How could I be such a monster you couldn't bring yourself to confide in me? I never forgot that night we shared, but when we met up again in Rome and you said nothing I thought you wanted to put it behind you, and I respected that—' And now I know why you said nothing, Santino added silently to himself as he gently lifted Kate's hands and held them between his. She wore the dazed expression of someone who had woken after a long sleep as she looked at him. 'I wish I'd been there for you,' he said, meaning it.

'You couldn't have known…'

She was defending him even now, after everything that had happened? He didn't deserve this tenderness. 'I wish I had known. I wish I could have helped you…' He felt a huge surge of relief to see her eyes slowly focusing, to see her coming back to him.

'Neither of us thought this could happen.'

'People in the situation in which we found ourselves rarely

do,' he said with a slow, half-sad, half-wry smile. 'You can't blame yourself for that. You can't blame yourself for anything.' Holding her hands firmly, he chafed them to bring the blood flowing back into her waxen fingers. 'I'm here for you now, Kate. Francesca's tiny brother has two parents, not one.'

'And you must be allowed to grieve too…'

'We'll do that together.' He held her gaze and as she smiled tremulously he felt nothing but massive relief. She hadn't understood that by talking about the child they had lost instead of shutting out the memories she could start to live again. This hidden sorrow explained so much about her. It explained everything.

'*L'angelo piccolo* is part of our lives, Kate, and nothing will ever change that. You will never be alone with this again. I give you my word.'

When the housekeeper tapped on the door then to see if there was anything else Signor Rossi needed before she went home he reassured her that he had everything he required. As she closed the door he turned back to Kate. 'I think you should try to sleep now. A bedroom has been prepared for you… Francesca knows where you are, and she asked me to be sure to tell you that she loves you and she is very excited about tomorrow.'

'Tomorrow?'

'Tomorrow,' he whispered against her lips. 'But now you must sleep Kate.'

'You're very kind.'

'I'm the father of your babies.' He held her gaze, and then, carefully drawing her to her feet, he steered her towards the door. 'We'll speak again in the morning when you've had some rest. If you need anything, anything at all, just call me. I'll be in the next room.'

Kate couldn't believe how long she had slept the next morning. Santino had already left for the studio by the time she got up.

'Signor Rossi tells me not to disturb you. He says you need to sleep,' Santino's housekeeper informed Kate as she served breakfast in the dining room. 'That is why I do not wake you up. Do not worry,' she insisted, making fanning motions with her hands when Kate started to fire questions at her. 'As soon as you are ready to leave for the studios I will call the car.'

'Ten minutes?' Kate held up her fingers.

The elderly housekeeper made a clucking sound with her tongue to show her opinion of rushing breakfast, but reassured Kate with an indulgent, if disapproving, 'Okay…'

Stopping off at the hotel for a change of clothes, Kate was relieved to find her suits had been returned. The car was waiting for her outside and she asked the driver to take every short cut he knew. She didn't want to be late for work. She didn't want to be away from Santino. She was desperate to see him again; desperate to know how he felt now he'd had time to sleep on everything she'd told him.

First impressions weren't good. His face was thunderous.

'What are you doing here?'

'My job,' she said defensively.

'You're supposed to be resting.'

Her tension eased as he ushered her aside.

'I could have managed without you for a day, Kate. You're more important than all this.' He made an impatient gesture.

'I'm fine. I can handle it.'

'I don't want you to handle it.'

His fiery Latin temperament was coming to the fore again, which prompted her to put a hand on his sleeve to reassure him. 'Thank you for last night, Santino,' she said gently, staring into his eyes.

'Thank you?' he said incredulously. 'Kate, will you stop this? Can you hear yourself?'

He drew her close in front of everyone.

'Don't do that,' she muttered against his chest. 'I might break down.'

'And about time too,' Santino said fiercely, kissing the top of her head.

'I've got work to do…' Kate was aware of the interest they were causing.

'Not for long.' But he released her.

What did he mean? Kate wondered. Had nothing changed? Perhaps Santino meant that as the weekend was fast approaching she would be leaving with Francesca very soon. It was foolish to expect more even if they had shared too much to ever be strangers again. But what were they, then?

She was soon swept up into the life of the studio and Caddy's few and always considerate demands on her time. Kate was glad of it, because work was the best therapy she knew.

She arranged for hot soup and panini, along with cheeses and a selection of pickles and fresh salad, to be brought to the room where Santino and his team were working. The place was buzzing and no one wanted to break off for lunch. They ate as they worked, firing questions, filling in story blocks… Kate loved it. She thrived on pressure. Hard work had always been her salvation. That was why Meredith had been right to get her out of the house. Everyone needed a focus and a goal, especially after a tragedy.

Santino's many glances warmed her, but Kate warned herself not to read too much into them. It was only natural he would show concern for the mother of his children, and especially after what she had told him.

When he finally brought the meeting to a close Kate didn't want to put Santino under any obligation to be with her, and quickly said to the room at large, 'I'll just go and type up my notes and then you can all have a copy by this afternoon—'

'No, I'm afraid not,' Santino told his team. 'That will have to wait, because Kate will be taking the rest of the day off.'

'I will? I don't need to convalesce,' Kate said discreetly as everyone filed out of the room. 'I appreciate your concern, but—'

'Stop it,' Santino warned sharply. 'You don't need to pretend with me, Kate. That's behind us now.'

'But my work…'

'I'm going,' he said, disregarding her comment. 'Are you coming with me?'

'I can't just walk out.'

'Why not?'

'Because people need me.'

'I need you.'

She wanted to believe him so badly.

'*Ciao,* Kate.'

'You're going?'

'That's right, Kate. I'm going. You can come with me, or you can stay here.'

He didn't want to play games with her any more. What she had told him about Francesca's twin had changed his whole outlook on life. They were joined now, and he wanted everything else out in the open too. It wasn't his way to sneak around having affairs that had to be kept quiet as if he were ashamed of them. He was in love with Kate. It was both a revelation to him and a source of great joy, and he wanted the whole world to know. 'What's the matter, Kate?' he asked her now. 'Are you scared?'

'Scared?'

'Yes, scared. Scared of feelings, scared of letting your feelings run away with you. Are you a coward now? Has the past beaten you, or are you ready to celebrate the life we have and move on?'

She looked shocked at first, and then as she cocked her head to look at him a small hesitant smile appeared on her lips. It made him go back for her. Taking her gently by the arms, he drew her in front of him. 'Kate,' he murmured, dipping his head to stare at her.

Slowly comprehension dawned in her eyes, and then they darkened.

'Can we go now?' he said dryly.

CHAPTER SIXTEEN

SANTINO had helped her to step past the barrier in her mind, Kate realised as he opened the front door to his apartment. Meredith and Caddy had been a wonderful source of strength, but with so many secrets locked inside her she had been stuck in a place she hadn't known how to get out of and it had taken something exceptional to set her free. Santino was exceptional in every way and as her lips parted to tell him as much he dipped his head and kissed her.

'Shall we move on?' he suggested, backing her into the hallway so he could close the door.

It really was very convenient to have a place in town, Kate thought wickedly, winding her arms around his neck. He kissed her again, more deeply this time, making her want him again. She could feel the heat rushing through her limbs as she kissed him back like a lover who had just discovered the other half of her soul.

Swinging her into his arms, Santino carried her into his bedroom where he laid her gently on the bed, but Kate's hunger was roused and she reached for him. She wanted to strip off his clothes. She wanted to see him naked. She wanted to feel his strong, warm body moving over her.

She had his shirt off in moments and then her hands raced

to deal with the buckle on his belt. But then her hectic breathing stuttered to a halt as Santino, now completely naked, stood looking down at her. He was magnificent. He was everything she could ever want in a man. Muscular and tanned, he was provocatively, brazenly sexual, like a gladiator from some ancient etching. She let her gaze linger on the wide spread of his shoulders and the rippling muscles on his torso. There was such power in his limbs, and such beauty. The shading of dark chest hair led her gaze below his waist to a place where even now she dared not look.

Completely unabashed, Santino stood astride, allowing Kate's heated gaze to rove over him. She relished the sight of his muscular thighs and beautifully shaped calves, and even his naked feet. He was like a flawless sculpture cast in bronze. It was so hard to keep her hands off him and stay on the bed, she wanted him so badly.

'Take off your clothes.'

Kate paused at the command, staring up at Santino, hardly able to draw breath for excitement.

'Take your clothes off…and do it slowly,' he instructed.

For a moment Kate was ashamed of her shabby suit. It was as if she were seeing it herself the first time. What was she wearing clothes like this for? she wondered as she tugged it off. Santino had made her see herself differently. The world was a brighter place, full of possibility…

'Slowly,' he reminded her.

She was ready to please him and she wanted to please him… She took particular care peeling off the sheer stockings she had on beneath her suit and was rewarded by Santino's sharp intake of breath as she revealed her moon pale thighs. Freeing the zip on her skirt, she slipped it off and tossed it aside. Her thin blouse came off quickly, and now she was only wearing briefs and a very flimsy bra that barely managed to contain the full swell of her breasts.

'Very, very slowly,' Santino instructed as Kate's hands moved up to the fastening at the back of her bra.

With a sigh she eased her shoulders and allowed her breasts to spring free. Her nipples were erect and blush pink and her breathing quickened when she saw the frank admiration in Santino's gaze. Having feasted his eyes he indicated that she should continue.

The wait was growing harder for both of them, just as he had intended. All that was left now were her tiny, white cotton briefs...

They came together like a force of nature, like wild beasts, with only one thought, one goal in mind, Kate stripping herself naked before Santino even had chance to hook his thumbs beneath the waistband of her briefs. They cried out repeatedly, urging each other on and there was no time for tenderness, or opportunity for finesse. There was only hunger and an aching need to prove again and again that they belonged to each other and always had.

'I love it when you speak to me in Italian,' Kate purred as Santino whispered wickedly in her ears. It made her reach for him again, and made her body undulate beneath him, tempting him on, luring him back, and it was only moments before Santino took her to a place where thought was no longer possible. And all the time he was kissing her and urging her on in his own language.

Closing her eyes, Kate concentrated on the sensation of having his skilful hands work her body like an instrument...positioning her, pleasuring her, providing her with everything any woman could ever want. The hard touch of him, his intimate touch, the most intimate touch of all allowed for nothing but pleasure, and at her request Santino thrust into her again.

But this time was different… This time Kate wanted Santino to fall with her and with a supreme effort of will she held back. Adjusting her position, she held him firmly in every way she knew how. His response was immediate. The hands gripping her flexed and he moaned.

'*Ti amo*, Kate… I love you.'

'And I love you too…'

And this time, just as she had wanted, they were both set free.

It was a long time before Kate was ready to admit to exhaustion, and when she did Santino held her close, kissing away the tears that had come to tremble on her lashes.

'What's wrong, *mio amore?*' he whispered. 'Why are you crying?'

'There's so much we don't know about each other. Is it only sex, Santino?' Her eyes raked his face, searching his soul. 'Because if it is, I would rather know now.'

'Kate, Kate…' He kissed away her tears. '*Ti amo, il mio Kate, io sono stato colpito dal darto dell'amore*… I love you with all my heart, my darling Kate. You are my heart's song, *il mio caro…*'

'But you don't know me…'

'I know you're always too hard on yourself. I know what Meredith told me about how distraught you were when your parents disowned you.'

'She shouldn't have.'

'Yes, she should,' he argued. 'Meredith loves you and only wants the best for you.'

'You?' She began to smile again to his relief.

'Of course,' he said, unable to curb his grin.

'And what about you, Santino? You're a man without a history, without a family—'

He went quiet.

'Tell me,' Kate insisted gently.

He turned to look at her. 'All right… I am man who was a boy living like a rat in the back streets of Rome. That boy is still with me, maybe he always will be with me, and that boy trusts no one…'

The temperature in the room seemed to drop and Kate could understand that Santino's difficulty in trusting anyone was founded upon who knew what horrors in his childhood. How could she blame him when she too had been so fearful of feelings?

He had never spoken about his childhood to anyone. Who would believe him if he had? Santino Rossi, the billionaire entrepreneur, a guttersnipe? Impossible, they would have said. He was associated in everyone's mind with the high-glamour world of film. If they only knew he was as much a creation of fantasy as a character in one of his films. He had invented himself and had always shunned pity or curiosity, believing it weakened him. And if there was one thing he had learned on the cold streets of Rome it was that he had to stay strong; strong, cold, and aloof, just like Kate…except for one night five years ago. And of course, now…

She came to him when he thought the weight of memories etched on his face must surely drive her away and, reaching out, she touched his face. This time he didn't pull back.

'I need your strength,' she whispered.

'I need yours too,' he admitted, surprising himself.

Kate woke first and found Santino asleep at her side. He looked even more beautiful when he was asleep, if such a thing were possible. The stubble on his face made him seem dark and dangerously forbidding like a pirate. A lock of inky black hair had caught on his eyelashes, and his sensual lips were curved in a contented smile like a child.

She loved him. Resting her chin on her hand, Kate smiled down at the man she loved, knowing that however incredible it might seem they had found each other again, and found in each other the answer to the pain in the past. Santino had told her about his mother never coming back and now she understood why he had grown up with such a loathing inside him. It was fear really, fear and agony he had brought with him from his childhood. There were no more secrets between them now.

'Kate?'

She hadn't realised Santino was awake or that she was crying silently. 'It's nothing,' she assured him. 'I'm just happy…'

Turning her face so she had to look into his eyes, Santino whispered again, '*Ti amo*, Kate…' He would never grow tired of telling her how much he loved her.

There were so many firsts. He had never declared his love for a woman before. But then he had never loved before Kate and Francesca had come into his life. He had never thought to find love, or to deserve it, or to have even the glimmer of a chance of building a family. Falling in love with Kate meant he could finally put his childhood behind him. It was that simple and that momentous. A lifetime of holding back on emotion made it difficult for him to express his feelings, but he was learning. And it was all thanks to Kate who had come back to him.

He felt a great swell of love for her as he took her into his arms. Their lips barely touched, the moment hanging as forgiveness and compassion flowed between them. There were no words because there was time ahead of them to talk and to explain and the present was for the healing power of love and for the start of a journey it would take a lifetime to complete.

'So do I take it I have a new assistant?' he murmured, his face creasing in a grin.

'Some people will stop at nothing to hire good staff.'

'I've never had to go quite this far before,' he admitted, gazing at the rumpled sheets.

She laughed and it was music to his ears. 'Are you nervous?'

'Of the job? No.'

'Of me, then?' he suggested.

'You?' Kate smiled into his eyes. 'You, I can handle…'

He laughed as she reached for him again and Kate was laughing too, with pleasure and excitement.

'Do you never get tired?' she asked him.

'Not when you're around,' he assured her, sinking deep.

He drank her eager cries into his mouth and it was only moments before she tumbled over the edge again.

Santino was laughing softly, Kate realised when she finally lay limp and spent in his arms. But before she had opportunity to chastise him he drew her on top of him.

'Enough?' he suggested, pulling a face of mock concern.

With what little remained of her strength Kate balled her hands into fists and pummelled them against Santino's chest. 'I've not nearly finished with you yet.'

'That's the kind of threat I appreciate,' he said, wasting no time in testing her claim.

It felt so right and so good. It was like making love for the very first time, and they went on until Kate truly was exhausted, and she knew there wasn't a single hunger or need that Santino hadn't catered for. And when he held her now he kissed her eyelids, her lips and her brow in homage to the woman Santino said he loved more than life itself.

* * *

It was getting late by the time they showered and dressed and Santino made them some food, a simple omelette, which they ate sitting side by side on bar stools in the kitchen. He wanted to reassure her. He could see now how clumsy he had been with all his talk of lawyers and contracts and divisions between them. There was a lot of bridge building to do and he wanted to complete it before he took Kate back to the *palazzo* where Francesca was waiting.

He needed the reassurance of Kate's body as she needed his, but there was so much more to their relationship. His life meant nothing to him without Kate at his side. And so he took the opportunity to tell her more about the past, stories he hadn't told anyone before. And once he had started he found it impossible to stop. It was like lancing a boil, and when he finally grew silent again she cupped his face in her hands and told him she loved him. It was all he had ever wanted.

When she made a move to go he made an executive decision. 'I'm going to ring Meredith and say we'll be back in the morning. He glanced at his watch and shrugged regretfully. 'I'm afraid you'll have to stay another night, Kate…'

He loved the way the smile crept slowly into her eyes and curved her lips. He loved it even more when she fell into his arms.

'So you'll come and work for me,' he teased later when they were entwined around each other in bed.

'You certainly need someone.'

'I certainly do,' he agreed, already wanting her again.

She drew a breath and closed her eyes, and he felt the ripple of response run right through her body as she melted against him.

'Who do I need?' he demanded roughly against her lips.

'Me?' she suggested as her eyes fluttered open. 'Definitely

me,' she said with confidence as he grew hard again between her hands.

'*Ti amo,* Kate…'

'I love you too, Santino…'

His heart soared. With Kate at his side the family he had always longed for was finally within his grasp. He was ready to love now, ready to commit his life to Kate, if she would have him.

He took her back to the *palazzo* in the morning where Francesca was waiting for them on the patio with Meredith.

'I hope you're all feeling like a walk today,' Santino said, stretching his muscular body.

'Is something special happening?'

Francesca looked hopeful and wary all at the same time, Kate thought.

'Maybe,' Santino said mysteriously. 'If you don't come with me you'll never know, will you?'

'Mummy can't walk in those clothes,' Francesca observed, glancing with disapproval at Kate's suit, which of course she had been forced to wear again.'

'Then we shall have to fix her up with some new ones…'

Which he had already, Kate discovered when Francesca insisted they go exploring in the dressing room attached to Kate's suite after breakfast.

Kate quickly changed into a casual outfit—jeans, jumper and sneakers. They were to meet Santino in the courtyard in ten minutes so there was no time to worry about who had paid for the new clothes now, though it made Kate smile to think Santino had judged her size so accurately—down to the last centimetre.

'No need to ask who's responsible for these,' she teased him as they all piled into the Range Rover, 'but I insist on paying for them.'

'I can always dock them from your first month's wages.'

'A whole wardrobe of new clothes from the kind of places you frequent? More like ten years' wages.'

'Ten years', then,' Santino said casually. 'I guess this means you'll have to stay on in Rome a lot longer than we thought?'

His lips tugged up at one corner as he turned his wicked stare on her, but as Francesca exclaimed with excitement Kate shot Santino a warning glance. Nothing was certain except they loved each other, nothing had been decided yet, the future was still a blank, and she didn't want to raise Francesca's hopes. 'Where are you planning to take us?' she said, determined to steer the conversation in a safer direction.

'Somewhere I hope you like,' Santino said enigmatically as he started the engine.

They had to duck down beneath a screen of bushes and try not to move a muscle for in the glade were several doe with their fawns, quite sturdy now at around six months old. And in the shadow of the trees keeping watch over his harem, a cinnamon-tinted buck tossed his antlers and sniffed the air…

'Does he know we're here?' Kate's mouth was almost touching Santino's ear lobe as she whispered to him, and when he turned to answer her she found their lips were almost touching. Their gaze met and held.

'No, we're downwind of him and quite safe.' He squeezed her hand and smiled, a warm, intimate smile that held her until the sound of leaves crunching underfoot as the deer walked away distracted her.

'Come on,' Santino said, springing to his feet, 'or we'll be late…'

'Late? Late for what?' Kate chased after him.

'Come on, Mummy, we have to hurry,' Francesca said, catching hold of Kate's hand to drag her along even faster.

'What have you two cooked up? And where's Meredith gone?' Kate said, suddenly realising her aunt had disappeared.

'She's gone ahead,' Santino explained, taking Kate's other hand to lead his little group deeper into the forest.

They walked until the trees thinned out and Kate could see a wooden fence with a gateway shaded by a rose-covered archway. Birds were singing in the trees, and the scent of freshly mown grass was in the air. Beyond a velvety swathe of emerald-green grass lay a beautiful old house set in spacious gardens with mullioned windows glittering benignly in the mellow light. 'What a beautiful home,' Kate exclaimed softly. 'Who lives here, Santino?'

'I thought you and Francesca might like to… Me too. How about it, Kate? What do you think? In a house this size we can be a real family.'

'Are you serious?' Kate searched his gaze.

'I never joke about investments,' he said dryly.

She might have believed him if he hadn't begun to smile. 'You're teasing me,' Kate said, beginning to smile too.

'Would I dare?'

There wasn't much Santino Rossi would not dare to do, Kate thought happily as Santino kissed her.

'Hurry up…everyone's waiting for us,' Francesca called back to them as she ran on towards a pathway that led up to the house.

'Everyone? What does she mean?' Kate turned to Santino.

'We'd better go and find out.'

'You two have been keeping secrets from me.'

'But I love surprises, don't you?'

The expression in Santino's eyes made Kate's heart pound

and as his gaze slipped to her lips she knew they'd better follow Francesca right away.

But Santino had other ideas.

It was a long, lingering kiss that was a pledge for the future and a promise for life.

'This could be our home, Kate… Just imagine it… This could be where we remember our little lost baby and where we make a home for Francesca; a home where she can grow up to be happy and strong like her mother. And perhaps in time it will be a home for more children to grow and thrive and love…'

Holding the little silver locket around her neck tightly in her hand Kate exchanged a look of understanding with Santino. She was certain now that all the things she cared about he would honour equally. They would share everything…sorrow, happiness, and everything else the future held. She would never be alone again. Neither of them would ever be alone again.

'It's a little cosier than the *palazzo*,' Santino admitted wryly, tilting his chin towards the house. 'Though we can use the *palazzo* too, if you like it… Well?' he said. 'What do you think, Kate?'

'I think I love you…'

'That's what I was hoping you would say.' Swinging her into his arms, he walked under the archway leading to their home.

As Santino carried her across the threshold a great cheer went up. And then Kate saw that everyone was crowded into the wood-panelled hallway from Caddy and Meredith, to the lady who made the tea on the set, and even the Italian couple who owned the restaurant where she and Santino had enjoyed their first meal together.

'You did all this for me?' She could hardly believe it.

'For you and for Francesca…' Reaching into the back pocket of his jeans, Santino brought out a small velvet-covered box. 'And now, because I want the whole world to know that I'm in love with you, I'm going to ask you a question in front of all these witnesses.'

'And embarrass me?'

'Almost certainly,' Santino agreed, wholly unrepentant.

Everyone held a collective breath as he flipped the lid on the tiny jewel case.

'Will you marry me, Kate Mulhoon?' he said, getting down on one knee.

Kate gasped as she looked at the large, clear blue Burmese sapphire surrounded with brilliant cut blue-white diamonds.

'You'd better say something,' Santino warned her, 'because if you don't I can't give Francesca her gift.'

'Then I'd better say yes... My answer's yes,' Kate declared happily so everyone could hear. 'I will marry you, Santino.'

'I haven't finished yet,' Santino warned when the cheers had died down. He made a signal and one of the crew dragged a large tin trunk into the middle of the hall.

'This is for you, Francesca,' he said. 'I hope you like it and find it useful.'

'What is it?' Francesca's eyes widened.

'Open it and see,' Santino advised, putting his arm around her mother's shoulders to draw her close.

It was the most comprehensively fitted-out tack box Kate had ever seen, with everything necessary to take care of a very special pony. 'How did you think of it?' she said, turning to Santino. 'It's such a wonderful idea.'

He shrugged. 'I just want us all to be happy.'

'Ever after,' Kate teased him.

'Let's leave fantasy to the film world,' Santino suggested as he stared deep into Kate's eyes. 'This is my reality, and it's the only reality I want.'

'A family?' Kate suggested tenderly.

'The greatest gift a man can have,' Santino agreed, meeting Kate's gaze before drawing her into his arms.

® HARLEQUIN®

Mediterranean
N I G H T S™

*Experience glamour, elegance, mystery and revenge
aboard the high seas....*

Coming in September 2007...

BREAKING ALL
THE RULES

by

Marisa Carroll

Aboard the cruise ship *Alexandra's Dream* for
some R & R, sports journalist Lola Sandler is
surprised to spot pro-golfer Eric Lashman.
Years after walking away from the pro circuit
with no explanation to the public, Eric now
finds himself teaching aboard a cruise ship.

Lola smells a career-making exposé...
but their developing relationship may
force her to make a difficult choice.

BILLI●NAIRES' BRIDES

Pregnant by their princes...

Take three incredibly wealthy European princes
and match them with three beautiful, spirited women.
Add large helpings of intense emotion and passionate
attraction. Result: three unexpected pregnancies—and
three possible princesses—if those princes have their way....

Coming in September:

THE GREEK PRINCE'S CHOSEN WIFE
by Sandra Marton

Ivy Madison is pregnant with Prince Damian's baby—
as a surrogate mother! Now Damian won't let Ivy go—after
all, he didn't have the pleasure of taking her to bed before....

Available in August:

THE ITALIAN PRINCE'S PREGNANT BRIDE

Coming in October:

THE SPANISH PRINCE'S VIRGIN BRIDE

REQUEST YOUR FREE BOOKS!

 HARLEQUIN *Presents*

2 FREE NOVELS
PLUS 2
FREE GIFTS!

YES! Please send me 2 FREE Harlequin Presents® novels and my 2 FREE gifts. After receiving them, if I don't wish to receive any more books, I can return the shipping statement marked "cancel." If I don't cancel, I will receive 6 brand-new novels every month and be billed just $3.80 per book in the U.S., or $4.47 per book in Canada, plus 25¢ shipping and handling per book and applicable taxes, if any*. That's a savings of close to 15% off the cover price! I understand that accepting the 2 free books and gifts places me under no obligation to buy anything. I can always return a shipment and cancel at any time. Even if I never buy another book from Harlequin, the two free books and gifts are mine to keep forever.

106 HDN EEXK   306 HDN EEXV

Name	(PLEASE PRINT)	
Address		Apt. #
City	State/Prov.	Zip/Postal Code

Signature (if under 18, a parent or guardian must sign)

Mail to the **Harlequin Reader Service®:**
IN U.S.A.: P.O. Box 1867, Buffalo, NY 14240-1867
IN CANADA: P.O. Box 609, Fort Erie, Ontario L2A 5X3

Not valid to current Harlequin Presents subscribers.

Want to try two free books from another line?
Call 1-800-873-8635 or visit www.morefreebooks.com.

* Terms and prices subject to change without notice. NY residents add applicable sales tax. Canadian residents will be charged applicable provincial taxes and GST. This offer is limited to one order per household. All orders subject to approval. Credit or debit balances in a customer's account(s) may be offset by any other outstanding balance owed by or to the customer. Please allow 4 to 6 weeks for delivery.

Your Privacy: Harlequin is committed to protecting your privacy. Our Privacy Policy is available online at www.eHarlequin.com or upon request from the Reader Service. From time to time we make our lists of customers available to reputable firms who may have a product or service of interest to you. If you would prefer we not share your name and address, please check here. ☐

HP07

When four bold, risk-taking women
challenge themselves and
each other...no man is safe!

Harlequin Blaze brings you

THE MARTINI DARES

A brand-new sexy miniseries from
award-winning authors

Lori Wilde
Carrie Alexander
Isabel Sharpe
Jamie Denton

DON'T MISS BOOK 1,

MY SECRET LIFE
by Lori Wilde

Available September 2007
wherever books are sold.